"Don't lo... **growled.**

"Like what?" Augusta asked.

His intense glance traveled up tanned legs, taking in the body beneath the water-soaked T-shirt and denim shorts. Desire pounded through him and his hands gripped the doorjamb as he looked up to see a delicate pulse beating madly under the creamy skin of her neck. His breath held as she moistened her lips, and he felt the heat in her golden eyes. "Like you need to kiss me as much as I need to taste you again."

She held his probing gaze and remained silent.

The lady was becoming too tempting. "You're going to have to tell me what you want," he said quietly. Was she willing to admit the attraction?

Augusta was oblivious to the cool water still splattering her clothes and heated skin. Her voice breathless with anticipation, she said, "I want you to kiss me."

He froze for a heartbeat. His surprise was overshadowed by fierce desire. Primitive urges swelled and every muscle in his body quivered with need as he hauled her into his arms.

Augusta answered the demand of his lips and reveled in the sinfully delicious sensations in every fiber of her being. This was a man who knew how to kiss, and she wanted it to go on forever. . . .

WHAT ARE *LOVESWEPT* ROMANCES?

They are stories of true romance and touching emotion. We believe those two very important ingredients are constants in our highly sensual and very believable stories in the *LOVESWEPT* line. Our goal is to give you, the reader, stories of consistently high quality that may sometimes make you laugh, sometimes make you cry, but are always fresh and creative and contain many delightful surprises within their pages.

Most romance fans read an enormous number of books. Those they truly love, they keep. Others may be traded with friends and soon forgotten. We hope that each *LOVESWEPT* romance will be a treasure—a "keeper." We will always try to publish

*LOVE STORIES YOU'LL NEVER FORGET
BY AUTHORS YOU'LL ALWAYS REMEMBER*

The Editors

Loveswept® 570

Marcia Evanick
Sweet Temptation

BANTAM BOOKS
NEW YORK · TORONTO · LONDON · SYDNEY · AUCKLAND

SWEET TEMPTATION

A Bantam Book / October 1992

If you would be interested in receiving protective vinyl
covers for your Loveswept books, please write to this address
for information:

> *Loveswept*
> *Bantam Books*
> *P.O. Box 985*
> *Hicksville, NY 11802*

ISBN 0-553-44132-9

Published simultaneously in the United States and Canada

PRINTED IN THE UNITED STATES OF AMERICA

OPM   0 9 8 7 6 5 4 3 2 1

To my daughter, Cassandra—
mischievous smiles,
daring courage,
and the ability to wrap the
world around her finger.
That's what my little girl is made of.

Love,
Mom

One

Garrison Fisher pulled the brim of his bush hat lower and leaned against the faded green wall of Hot Springs' run-down bus station. His interest was completely taken by what was easily the most fascinating object in the room—a very female derriere. He couldn't tell much about the rest of the woman because she was kneeling on a wooden bench and facing a young boy sitting behind her, but the sweet view was enough to start his heart pounding and desire flowing. Crossing his ankles, he tried to figure out what she was doing.

She seemed to be writing or drawing. Her beige tweed skirt, stretched over luscious curves, reached down to her knees. Off-white stockings clung to her calves, and a pair of low-heeled beige pumps barely hung on to her toes as she bobbed her head at something the boy was saying. Garrison groaned and pulled his hat even lower. Hours of working under the sun and digging in fossil beds had finally taken their toll. How else could he explain the sweet temptation of a prim business suit?

Muttering a few choice words that his mother would have washed his mouth out for using, he glanced away toward the far wall and saw a woman surrounded by piles of luggage. She had to be Augusta Faye Bodine.

What had he ever done to deserve such a fate? Sure, he missed the faculty meeting in April, where everyone voted to allow a children's book writer and illustrator to join his summer dig. But he found the meetings so boring and unproductive, and his time was better put to use with more rewarding endeavors, such as helping his students or pursuing a very understanding female. Besides, Augusta Faye Bodine hadn't been on the agenda; if Garrison had known that Walt Newman, the head of the department, would bring her up and bulldoze everyone, he would have found time to attend. The final decision affected *his* life, after all, not Newman's.

But Newman had held a grudge against him since his seventh article appeared in *Smithsonian Magazine* last year and Newman's was rejected. Newman was probably still chuckling over the disaster he'd caused. Augusta Faye Bodine turned out to be the granddaughter of Bertram Fremont, the dean of the College of Sciences at the University of Montana, and Old Iron-Pants Fremont hadn't been happy with the vote.

A couple of weeks after the meeting, the dean had gone hunting for Garrison and found him in a dusty, dimly lit storage room on campus, right in the middle of a poker game with the professor of medieval literature, the women's basketball coach, and three students. Fremont had blown a gasket when he saw that the kitty consisted of tyrannosaurus teeth. It had been Garrison's bad luck to be raising a femur of a pachycephalosaurus when the dean had walked in.

Fremont had cleared the room of everyone except Garrison and explained, in great detail, what would happen to a very important part of his anatomy if one hair on his precious granddaughter's head was harmed. It was the first Garrison had learned of the matter.

The dean was about as pleased as Garrison. It seems his darling granddaughter skipped by him and went straight to Newman. The vote went through without anyone connecting Augusta Bodine with Bertram Fremont. Permission was granted and the plans had been laid before Fremont was notified of the decision. Fremont would have rather seen his granddaughter carried off by cutthroat pirates than place her in Garrison's care for six weeks.

Garrison shuddered at the thought of having a belle from Georgia under his feet for the next six weeks. Fossil beds weren't any place for the inexperienced. The elements were harsh, the land unforgiving, and the odds stacked in favor of disaster. Accidents could happen within a blink of the eye, and if death had a calling card, it would be found in an excavation site. Garrison had witnessed one visit from the grim reaper while on a dig many years earlier and vowed never to allow the demon within fifty miles of his camp. Every one of his students and the visiting paleontologists on his crew had knowledge of camping and survival skills.

Baby-sitting some naive kiddie writer ranked right up there with having a root canal without novocaine. He couldn't care less if she was the dean's granddaughter or even the president's. Not only didn't she belong at the dig, he didn't want her there.

Garrison stared at the impatient-looking woman and her ten pieces of matching luggage and shuddered. She had to be Fremont's grandchild. She seemed the right age, and the family resemblance was remarkable. Why Fremont had gone all protective over her was a mystery to Garrison. With her stubborn jaw and narrow-eyed stare, dear, sweet Augusta, as Fremont had referred to her, could scare a Pteranodon.

Garrison pushed his hat back and gave the luscious tush one last lingering look before slowly making his way toward Augusta. He gave a silent prayer of thanks that she didn't arouse him as sweet temptation did. The next six weeks were going to be pure hell as it was. He didn't need the added burden of lust thrown in.

Augusta Bodine looked up from the sketch she had just finished for her new friend and watched as the long-limbed man walked across the station. She hadn't known anyone else had entered the bus depot. That wasn't unusual though. Whenever she started to draw, she stopped noticing the world around her. She got to her feet and yanked down her skirt, then frowned when the man, in a deep-timbred voice, addressed the other woman as Augusta Bodine.

"Do I look like an *Augusta* to you?" the woman snapped.

"Excuse me, I'm Augusta Bodine. Are you Garrison Fisher?" He heard the words spoken in a soft southern drawl that was as out of place in Montana as mint juleps and hush puppies.

Garrison spun around on his heel and looked down, way down. The top of Augusta Faye Bodine's head reached his chest. Huge golden eyes gazed questioningly up at him. Silky brown hair that swung around her shoulders caught the reflection of the overhead lights. The white silk blouse underneath her suit boasted a huge bow. She was better-looking from the front than from the rear. She was gorgeous, and every inch of her shouted *lady*. Garrison swallowed hard. "You're Augusta Faye Bodine?"

A radiant smile lit her face as she stuck out her hand. "Yes, and you must be Dr. Fisher. I've read some of your work. Remarkable."

Garrison gazed at the delicate hand as if it would bite him. Sweet temptation was going to be his camp guest for the next six weeks! She'll never survive. Hell, *he'll* never survive. He wiped his palm down his thigh and glared at his work-roughened hand. His nails were trim but embedded with dirt, and the palm was callused. He might as well give her a taste of what lay ahead. He reached out and shook her hand. Hard.

Augusta smiled and tightened her grip.

Surprise flared in him. Under the prim business suit the lady was full of spunk. "Are you sure you're a kids' writer?"

"I won the Bo-Peep Award two years in a row."

She took back her hand and refused to study the damage.

"The Bo-Peep Award?"

"It's a very prestigious childrens' book writer's award." Augusta always enjoyed watching adults swallow that piece of information. The name sounded as phony as a three-dollar bill, but receiving it was the high point of her career so far.

As Garrison burst out laughing, Augusta studied the man she'd heard so much about. His jaw was unshaven and his hair could have used a trim several weeks before. Sparkling white teeth contrasted with his tanned features. Dr. Fisher obviously spent a great deal of time outdoors. Faded jeans, tattered sneakers, and a T-shirt depicting a brontosaurus ridiculously trying to hide behind a tree and bearing the caption WE'RE NOT EXTINCT, WE'RE HIDING gave him the appearance of a college student rather than a professor. At a closer look she guessed he wouldn't see thirty-five again. "Are you sure you're Dr. Garrison Fisher, renowned paleontologist?"

His laughter immediately stopped, and he said, "Touché." Then he glanced over to where her huge green nylon duffel bag and a briefcase sat on the ground beside the wooden bench. "Where's the rest of your luggage?"

"That's it."

"All of it?" he asked incredulously.

"Dr. Newman told me to pack light and that you would be providing me with a tent, sleeping bag, and anything else I would need. I was to bring only clothes and a pair of hiking boots."

Garrison walked over to the bag and picked it

up. The muscles in his forearm bulged. "What in the hell did you pack, bricks?"

She retrieved the briefcase and waved good-bye to the little boy. "Don't be ridiculous. Would you like me to carry the bag?"

His reply was muffled as he strode through the depot. Augusta had to smile. Dr. Fisher was as outdated as his beloved dinosaurs. He would carry her luggage in his teeth before allowing her to lift the bag one inch off the floor. As if she could! She'd give up her spring cotillion tickets before admitting that the bus driver had to carry it inside the bus station for her.

Her dear granddaddy had warned her about the legendary doctor. It went against Fremont's better sense to allow her to be in the same state as Dr. Fisher, let alone in his camp. He even went as far as offering to arrange a trip to another dig, and she could name the site. Augusta had to take a firm stand against him. She had purposely not mentioned the family connection in her letter to Dr. Newman. She didn't want to obtain permission by favoritism. She had wanted to earn the right to accompany Dr. Fisher and his students. And she had.

She needed to be on an actual dig to fully understand and appreciate the significance of finding something over sixty-five-million years old if she was going to write about it. Dr. Fisher's annual dig had been her first choice. The doctor had the reputation of being the best. It was even rumored throughout the field that the doctor could smell a buried dinosaur bone. Add that to the fact that Dr. Fisher was the blight of her grandfather's existence, and the temptation to witness the paleontologist in action was too great to ignore.

Sometimes her family was the blight of her existence. Not only was she the youngest grandchild, and still considered the baby of the family at the age of twenty-eight, she had been named after Granddaddy's dear departed wife, Augusta.

Her family was constantly placing obstacles in her career path. Coming from a long line of intellectuals and downright geniuses was a curse. She didn't fit in. Everyone had her life planned since the day she was christened in the old Methodist church in historic Savannah. She was to have completed her Ph.D. by now, get married to a genius within a year, and bear two perfect little geniuses who would continue the untainted bloodline. A great disappointment to her family, she had only a bachelor's degree and no prospects—or any inclinations—of obtaining a genius for a husband.

Augusta walked up to the Jeep and placed her briefcase in the back with her luggage and countless boxes and bags. Garrison had obviously spent the morning shopping. Sliding into the passenger seat, she glanced at the tow-away–zone sign above the vehicle. From what she'd seen of Hot Springs as the bus had driven through it, she didn't think the town could afford a police force, let alone a tow truck.

Garrison changed the gear into reverse, refusing to glance again at the delicious curve of Augusta's calves. He was backing out the Jeep when he noticed Augusta was having difficulty with her seat belt. Hell, he didn't even know if it was still working. He jammed on the brakes and reached for the faded nylon strap. The back of his hand brushed her lap as he swept the strap across her and snapped it in place.

A delicate shiver of awareness slid down her back at the close contact. Granddaddy had warned her of the doctor's arrogance, disrespectful ways, and his brilliance. But in all the conversations they had regarding Dr. Fisher, at no time did Granddaddy mention the fact that he radiated pure male dominance. If Garrison were a dinosaur, he would be the dominant male of the herd. He would have every female fighting over the privilege of bearing his baby. Which brought up a very interesting question. "Did dinosaurs mate for life?"

Garrison's foot slipped off the clutch. Tumbling from her lips, the word *mate* sounded so provocative. Whenever he and his colleagues and students used that term, it had always meant the survival of the species and nothing more. "No. What prompted that question?"

"Just curious." She smiled and waved to a car going around them. Garrison's stalled Jeep was blocking the street.

Her smile was trouble, her enticing tush was sweet temptation, and her questions were lethal. Augusta wasn't only inexperienced at roughing it, she was a sexy, desirable lady. It was the worst possible combination. Garrison's hands gripped the steering wheel. "I'm turning this Jeep around and dropping you back at the bus station."

"Why?"

"The Boneyard is no place for a woman." It was

the first thing that came to mind. He knew it was sexist, but he was becoming desperate. There was no way he would explain the effect she was having on him.

"I understand there are at least four other females at the site."

"Three are college students and the fourth is a paleontologist from Princeton."

"Well, they are women, aren't they?"

"They're all trained and well equipped to handle the rough life at the Boneyard."

"I'm aware that it won't be a garden party." She politely nodded to a passing car and ignored Garrison's snort. She hadn't made it all this way to be turned back at the last minute. Her voice deepened with determination. "Dr. Newman *and* the university have already agreed to allow me to stay."

Garrison uttered an oath and glanced back at the bus station.

"Don't even think about it, Doc. I'm not getting back on a bus." She nervously ran her sweating palms down her skirt and issued the greatest threat she could think of. "If you don't allow me to stay, both my publisher and I would sue the university for breach of promise."

Garrison narrowed his eyes at her. "I don't take kindly to threats."

"Then I suggest you live up to your end of the deal."

He flashed her a predatory smile. "Are you referring to my new assignment of baby-sitting you?"

Augusta clenched her teeth. "I can assure you,

Dr. Fisher, I haven't needed a sitter since I was eight."

Garrison noisily shifted into gear and tore off down the street. "You have one now, Augusta Faye. The Boneyard and *everyone* in it is my responsibility. When I say stop, you stop. When I say go, you go. When I issue an order, I expect you to follow it. To the letter."

"Well, I've never!"

Garrison shot off the main road and headed out of town. "Well, you have now, sweetcakes." He said the last word with a sneer. "I guarantee that when I shove you back on the bus six weeks from now, you will be in one piece."

Understanding dawned on Augusta. He wasn't upset that she was a woman or even the dean's granddaughter. Garrison was concerned with her safety. "Dr. Fisher, let me assure you that my intelligence is above average and I'm secure enough with myself to accept advice from someone with more experience. I might be adventurous, but I'm not a risk taker. If you say something is danger- ous, rest assured I won't doubt you."

Garrison shot her a hard look before turning his attention back to the road.

The surrounding area was as different from Georgia as one could get. Augusta was used to lush mountains and forests, and here she saw only miles of gray hills. What did you expect, Gus? she chided herself. Dinosaur bones popping up poolside at the Hyatt Regency?

Hanging on to the dashboard, Augusta risked a peek at the speedometer and bit her lip. It read zero. The darn thing was broken. How could anyone drive a vehicle with a broken speedometer? She shifted her gaze to the endless road in front of them. At one time it might have been paved, but now it looked as though the air force had practiced bombing runs on it. But driving with amazing skill, Garrison managed to avoid all the larger holes.

Augusta chanced a desperate move ten minutes later. She removed one hand from the dashboard and dug through her purse until she located her sunglasses. With a triumphant smile she slipped them on and looked at Garrison. His frown seemed less intense. "I'm sorry," she said with a sigh.

Garrison turned the wheel sharply to the left to avoid a crater. "About what?" He glanced at her and for the first time in his six years at the university he could sympathize with Fremont. Augusta looked as delicate as a ripe Georgia peach.

"I found out that you hadn't voted with the rest of the department on my joining your dig."

"In the six years I've been working these hills, I have only once allowed someone who wasn't qualified to stay there."

"Who was that?"

"My ex-fiancée," he growled. "She managed to make it an entire three days before packing it in and calling it quits."

Augusta could tell by the tone of his voice that he didn't want to discuss his ex-fiancée. "Once we get to the camp, you can pretend I'm not even there."

"No way, lady."

She had thought it seemed like a reasonable

compromise. She'd stay out of his hair and complete her research while he got on with his work. "Why not?"

"Because you're my responsibility. You will never be more than ten feet away from me."

Augusta sputtered with indignation. "I don't need or *want* a keeper, Dr. Fisher."

"Have you ever been camping before?"

"For four weeks in Alaska, last summer."

His gaze quickly ran from the top of her head to her scuff-free beige pumps. "In a tent?"

"Cabin." Hearing his moan, she added, "A primitive cabin. It had an outhouse out back and no electricity."

"Then our Porta Potti will make you feel right at home."

Her chin rose an inch. "I believe I will manage."

Most *ladies* would run in terror, Garrison thought. "Ever run across a rattler?"

"As in snake?"

He noticed the way she tried to suppress her faint trembling. Rattlesnakes scared the hell out of him, too. "We have them. I've already spotted two this summer."

"I'll keep it in mind." *And probably in my nightmares too.*

"You do that."

Augusta wasn't worried about the doctor being strapped to her side during her stay. She figured he would be bored with her within a day or two, just as soon as he realized that all she wanted to do was draw and follow the crew around.

When she hadn't spoken in a while, Garrison glanced at her and saw a smile of amusement curving her lips. "You don't remind me of any of my professors," she said.

"I'm sure I'm not any different from them."

She chuckled. "You're different all right."

"How?"

"The way you dress and talk. I bet you don't even own a suit, do you?"

Garrison scowled. "I happen to own two."

"When was the last time you wore one?"

He swerved around a hole and tried to remember. The last time was when he and Catherine had attended some boring dinner party given by the head of the physics department. Catherine had dragged him from one dinner party to the next during their six-month engagement. He had hated it, and ended up hating Catherine in the process. He didn't hate her any longer. It had taken him a while to understand her dilemma. She had been in love with an image, an image he could never become. She had wanted glamour and social standing, things that didn't matter to him. He wanted to ignite the spark of knowledge in his students' eyes, feel the fossilized bones of a once-magnificent beast in his hands and understand how this creature lived. Achieving these goals meant a hard life, and Catherine could not live it. He hadn't worn a suit since that dinner party. "It's been about two years."

Augusta smiled. "I bet your students love you."

"Because I don't wear a suit?"

"No, because you don't conform."

Garrison's scowl deepened. "I hope to hell you're wrong. I hope they respect me because of my knowledge and my willingness to share it, not because I prefer jeans to flannel trousers."

Augusta stared at his profile. The man had another passion besides dinosaurs, and it was teaching. Filled with newfound respect, she said, "As I told you, you don't remind me of any of my professors."

He shot her a quick glance before returning his attention to the treacherous road. Somehow he felt he had just been given a great compliment.

As silence filled the Jeep once more, Augusta stared off into the distance. Her interest was captured by a dim flash of color from afar. She studied the specks and realized what she was seeing were multicolored tents of assorted sizes. As they drove closer, she picked out the infamous Porta Potti, half a dozen other vehicles, and a couple of clotheslines strung between tents from which shirts, pants, shorts, and towels were flapping.

Garrison whipped the Jeep off the road and headed straight toward the camp. After a couple of bone-jarring bounces he parked the shuddering Jeep behind a huge tent and killed the engine. "Here we are, lady. Home sweet home."

Augusta slowly climbed out of the vehicle and was amazed to find all her limbs were still working. She glanced around the deserted area. "Where is everyone?"

"Out in the field," he said, swinging out of the jeep. He lifted down her bag and headed for a green tent. She grabbed her briefcase and followed. He unzipped the flaps and shoved the bag inside. "This one is yours."

She looked inside and saw a folding cot, a rolled-up blue sleeping bag, and a lantern. All the comforts of home, she thought, summoning a smile. "Thanks, Doc Fisher."

"Since we're going to be neighbors"—he nodded toward an identical tent less than six feet away—"why don't you call me Garrison."

"Only if you call me Augusta instead of lady."

The tent on the other side of his was the biggest one in the camp. Its entire front open, it was obviously being used as the office. The tent on the other side of hers was evidently the kitchen. Assorted smaller tents were assembled to the right, and three newer nylon tents were grouped to the left.

"Didn't anyone ever give you a nickname or something?" Garrison asked.

"And suffer Bertram's wrath?"

Garrison chuckled at her use of the dean's first name. No one ever called Bertram Fremont anything besides Dr. Fremont, Dean Fremont, or just a plain respectful sir. "Did he name you?"

"No, but Mom named me after her mother."

He nodded his head in understanding. She was named after Fremont's late wife. "Augusta's a pretty big mouthful for a little slip of a thing like you."

She was unsure if she should take offense. The way it rolled off his tongue, it almost sounded like a compliment.

"Since I have a reputation to protect when it concerns ol' Bertram, from now on I'm going to call you Gus."

A trace of a smile touched her lower lip. Garrison had picked the secret name she used when talking to herself. "Suit yourself."

Garrison's gaze was focused on the smile and the softest, most enticing lips he had ever seen. "Get changed, put on sunblock, and some of that lip protector and we'll go introduce you to the rest of the crew." He turned on his heel and headed back toward the Jeep.

Five minutes later Augusta, dressed in suitable clothes, rezipped her tent flaps and backed right into Garrison's hard body. Her cry of surprise filled the unoccupied camp. "Lord, don't sneak up on a person like that."

"I was only standing here." He had been walking out of the office when he noticed her bent over outside her tent. The tush that guaranteed to cost him hours of sleep was now encased in khaki-colored shorts. A deep purple T-shirt clung to her every luscious curve, a pair of brand-new sturdy hiking boots graced her feet, and her hair was pulled back into a ponytail. She looked adorable. Dinosaurs will be shaking off millions of years of dirt and sandstone to have the privilege of being discovered by her. "Where's your hat?"

"I didn't bring one."

With her fair complexion, she was going to fry under the relentless sun that beat down on the Boneyard. He walked over to his tent and disappeared inside. He was back in an instant and slapped an old Giants baseball cap on top of her head. "Wear it." Refusing to gaze again at her, he walked over to the office.

Augusta pulled her ponytail through the opening in the back and settled the cap more firmly on her head. After slipping on her sunglasses, she followed. Without looking directly at her, Garrison handed her a small instrument with a hammer on one end and a pick on the other, a nylon tote bag, and a filled canteen. Without a backward glance or saying a word he headed out into the vast emptiness. Augusta tested the weight of the hammer in her hand and contemplated the distance to his retreating back. With a wistful smile she followed him into the sunlight.

Two

During the half-hour trek over sandstone hills and valleys, Garrison grudgingly indicated points of interest. But he was always there to offer a hand down a slippery slope or up a steep incline. The Boneyard was a walking portrait of nature's ruthlessness. Miles of gray hills, dry creek beds, and endless dust greeted her. Signs of past digs were marked with sun-bleached flags or sticks with torn pieces of material fluttering in the breeze. The man-made craters blended in with the natural landscape. Vultures soared above the uneven terrain, searching for their next meal. Augusta had to shake the feeling they were watching her.

When they reached the present dig site, Augusta saw a group of scruffy-looking young men and women busily brushing, pounding on, or carefully chipping at a huge mass of bones. They looked like a cluster of vultures viciously picking at the remains of some poor dead beast. Gray dust covered their faces and their clothes. She picked out the four females and counted five male students. As soon as Garrison made his appearance, their faces lit up with eager-to-please expressions.

She watched as Garrison hunched down next to a student wearing a straw hat and studied whatever he had uncovered. His deep voice mixed with the enthusiastic questions and replies the students were bombarding him with. Dr. Fisher was in his element surrounded by students hanging on to his every word and sixty-five-million-year-old fossils. This was what she came to capture on paper. Only problem was all her art supplies were back at the tent.

She took a few cautious steps toward a large rock and looked around for any sign of a rattler before sitting down. After a few curious and at least one hostile glance from the students, she was ignored, which was fine by her. She wanted the time to study the group at work.

Augusta dug through the tote bag and realized it must have belonged to Garrison's ex-assistant. If the stories were to be believed, Alysia had posed nude for some men's magazine, using the fossil beds as the backdrop. By the end of the shoot she was madly in love with the photographer and went with him when he returned to Chicago. Garrison was left without a qualified assistant.

In the bag, sunblock, flares, and a small first-aid kit competed with notepads, chewed-on pencils, and a fuchsia and turquoise striped bikini bottom. Curiously, the top of the bathing suit was missing. Augusta looked away from the microscopic bottom dangling from her fingertip to Garrison's back. The doctor was proposing more questions to the students than he was answering. She shook her head, placed the scrap of material back into the bag, and dug out a notepad and a stubby pencil. Soon she was busily sketching the look of determination and intelligence etched on one student's face.

"Augusta?" Garrison brushed off his hands and stood. The woman was destined to drive him crazy. He walked the few feet over to her and deepened his voice. "Gus!" Huge golden eyes rose in confusion. Her lower lip was pink and moist from her having chewed on it. A fierce desire to smooth away the hurt his rudeness caused made his fingers tremble. He shoved his hands into his pockets. "Don't you want to be introduced to the crew?"

She quickly closed the pad and stood up. He didn't have to sound as though she had been avoiding the meeting. He was the one who had disregarded her for the past fifteen minutes. "Of course, I was just waiting for you to remember your manners." With ladylike grace she brushed off her derriere and cautiously stepped over a huge bone to get closer to the waiting students.

Garrison combatted the shame of knowing she was right. He should have made the introductions when they first arrived and explained a little of what they were doing instead of being swept up in the crew's enthusiasm. He couldn't help it. Listening and seeing the students' fascination at unearthing something that was seventy million years old always brought back memories of how ecstatic he'd been when he'd dug up his first find. It was like

Christmas and opening the brightly wrapped present Aunt Eleanor always brought him. He knew it was probably some hideous sweater, but there was a chance it could be something wonderful. Like three years ago when she surprised him with a set of twelve dinosaur rubber stamps and five assorted-color ink pads. The stamps were lined up neatly on his desk at the university and had become his trademark when grading papers. Still, the fact that the kids were exposing a triceratops, a dinosaur abundant around that area, didn't give him the right to be remiss as a host.

"Everyone, I would like you to meet our guest for the next six weeks, Augusta Bodine."

Augusta smiled. "Hello."

"Are you a paleontologist?"

"No."

"Why are you here then?"

Augusta looked at the dirty-faced woman and smiled. "I write and illustrate children's books and my editor would like me to try my hand at dinosaurs." A male student snorted in disbelief.

Garrison shot the boy a hard look.

One student asked, "Are you going to do it about how dinosaurs lived?"

"No. I've read countless children's books on the subject and I find the facts vary from book to book. Some books portray them as huge monstrous creatures that devoured everything in their paths, and others as docile brainless beasts who barely had the intelligence to eat plants to survive."

Every student stared openmouthed at Garrison as he pushed the brim of his hat up his forehead and took on a obstinate stance. Augusta had unknowingly touched a very sensitive nerve. No one called his dinosaurs brainless and got away with it.

"I decided not to center on the dinosaurs themselves, but on the people who literally dig them up. In other words, you guys."

"Us?"

"Paleontologists."

"But we're not paleontologists yet," one student complained.

"I know, but you're very important to the story. I want to explain how a person becomes a paleontologist. All the hard work and studying you do." She smiled. "And that you don't necessarily have to be a boy to go digging for dinosaurs."

Three female faces lit up, and the students excitedly asked Augusta questions faster than she could answer. She had won over the group without even trying.

Garrison glanced at Harry Lentel, the student who had snorted, and noticed his hostile gaze directed at Augusta. Harry was always the odd man out. Obviously Augusta's charming presence hadn't won him over yet. He glanced at his watch. There were a couple of hours of daylight left before they would head back to the camp. "Caroline, why don't you explain to Augusta what we're trying to accomplish here?"

"Come on, Augusta," Caroline said, yanking Augusta closer to the triceratops.

"Ben, you're in charge here while I'm gone." Garrison pointedly gazed at Augusta's back, indicating to the student that he was responsible for

Augusta's safety. "I want to check something out. I'll be back in about two hours."

Augusta turned away from the engrossing skeleton to watch Garrison walk off. He was still obviously upset with having been delegated her *baby-sitter.* At least she wouldn't have to worry about being continually within ten feet of him as he promised. He was already at least fifty yards away and showed no sign of stopping.

"Ms. Bodine, look at this."

Augusta turned back to the group of students and smiled at the young man holding out a small bone. "Please, call me Augusta."

"See you tomorrow, Augusta."

Augusta smiled as the last of the students left the mess tent, and headed for their tents for the night.

"They seem quite naive, don't they?" Garrison said.

"No, they're young, that's all."

"They think they can change the world."

"Maybe they can." She looked over at Garrison and wondered what finally happened that started him talking. He had been quietly sitting in a canvas deck chair with his feet propped up on a bench all evening. His dark eyes seem to have followed her every move. "I didn't notice this trait of yours this morning."

A frown pulled at his mouth. "What trait?"

"Quiet, reserved. You know, sitting on the sideline, watching things happen."

"That's because it's not one of my qualities."

"Tonight it was."

"No, I was observing, that's all." He picked up a rock with the fossilized impression of a leaf and passed it from hand to hand. He regretted giving up cigarettes last year; the taste of one always helped him think better. "You handle yourself well with the kids."

"Did you think I wouldn't?"

"Being related to Fremont, you must have inherited some of *his* traits."

"I know about Bertram's reputation with the students and faculty, but he's a marshmallow underneath that crusty exterior."

Garrison chuckled at the thought of old man Fremont as a marshmallow. "If you say so."

She washed out her coffee cup, dried it, and put it away in a metal cabinet. "I must commend you on how well-run the camp is." Maybe he was expecting some type of praise from her.

"Thanks, but your name has been added to the cooking roster anyway."

Augusta crossed her arms. "I'll have you know, I can cook."

"Southern fried chicken, black-eyed peas, and pecan pie aren't on the menu."

"Is there a reason you're being so nasty toward me, or is this your normal personality?"

Garrison narrowed his eyes and the rock stilled. "I'm waiting for the prima donna to appear." She was a lady from the top of her freshly brushed hair to the tips of her dust-free hiking boots. When he had rejoined the group of students earlier, he had been shocked to discover Augusta sitting in the gray dirt chipping away at the sandstone covering a triceratops's pubis. She had been covered in dust and enjoying herself. Within minutes of returning to camp she had washed up, changed, and had her laundry hanging on a line that had mysteriously been strung between her tent and his. Augusta was taking to camp life like a fish to water, and it was unnerving him. He wanted her demanding a ride back into town to catch the next bus out of there. Sweet temptation was settling in for the haul, and he was afraid he wouldn't be able to resist the allure. Ladies and the Boneyard didn't mix. Hell, hadn't that point been nailed home more than two years ago by Catherine?

"You'll have one hell of a wait." To think she was actually starting to like the guy. The students put him on a pedestal as if he were equal to Zeus, and even the paleontologists from Princeton had excitedly conversed with him on their find of the day. They had thought they'd found some bones of a young troödon, which would have been a great find, but they unearthed only a metatarsal and a humerus of a microvenator. Garrison might be God's gift to the dinosaurs, but he was beginning to grate on her nerves.

He smiled in spite of himself. Her spunk was showing again. "Tsk, tsk. Such language coming from a lady."

"There's nothing wrong with being a lady," she snapped. They might as well clear the air her first night in camp. There was no sense in his carrying a grudge through the weeks to come, or her trying to illustrate the camaraderie of paleontologists during a dig when she was living in the Boneyard from hell.

He flashed her a predatory smile. "No, there isn't. I happen to like ladies." He studied the delicate curve of Augusta's cheek and thought that she looked as fragile as a baby duckbill.

"Just not independent ladies, right?"

"Especially independent ladies."

Augusta's heartbeat quickened and her mouth went dry. The look in his eyes was pure heat.

"To be on the safe side though, you're still my responsibility for the next six weeks."

"I really don't think that's necessary."

"I don't think your independence would stop a rattler from sinking its fangs into your shapely calf." He gazed at her delectable legs.

Augusta refused to acknowledge the stare or the jolt of awareness tingling up her leg. "It would be my fault for disturbing one, not yours."

"Would your independence prevent you from getting lost out there?"

"I know how to read a compass."

"With a rattler hanging from your leg?"

She tried to suppress the horrible image and failed. "You're just trying to scare me."

He slowly placed the rock on the table and stood. "I succeeded too, didn't I?" he took three steps and blocked her against the table without touching her.

"Why?" She raised huge golden eyes to examine his face as his powerful hands gripped the table on either side of her.

Temptation was mere inches away. He wanted to taste her mouth to see if it was as sweet as he imagined. The simple fact that she was a lady stopped him. "I want you to tell me you want to leave."

She shook her head. "I don't want to leave."

"What would you do if I picked you up and carried you away to my tent for a night of wild passion?"

He was trying to scare her off again, but this time he was using something more dangerous than a rattler. There was no way she would allow him to know how intrigued she was by the possibility. "Would I be a willing participant in this wild night or just some insignificant player?"

Outraged, he sputtered, "Insignificant player!"

She smiled innocently.

"How do you have a wild night of passion with an insignificant player?" he asked.

"I haven't the foggiest idea. You were the one spouting threats of wild passion."

"It takes two willing people to have wild passion, not one person. Don't they teach you Georgia belles anything?"

Offended by his slur of her home state, she managed to stare down her nose while still looking up at him. "They taught us that a *gentleman* shouldn't make threats against a lady and that scare tactics are crude."

She pointedly glared at his arms blocking her against the table. He slowly dropped them and stepped back. "Scare tactics?"

"Isn't that what your latest threat was, another tactic to have me running back into town?"

She was magnificent when riled, her golden eyes darkening to the color of his favorite beer. "It wasn't a threat; it's a distinct possibility if you stay here." He moved closer to her and hungrily gazed at her mouth. She was forbidden fruit. Even when he was a little boy he always wanted what every adult told him he couldn't have.

Augusta stilled at the heat of his body. He was either a very good actor or he was serious. She gazed at his mouth and wondered how he would kiss. Would it be with the arrogance and strength she knew he possessed, or would it be soft and gentle, like his touch when he handled delicate fossils? With a shock she realized she wanted him to kiss her. It was the worst thing she could want. Garrison was known for causing trouble across the campus and half the state of Montana. He didn't play by anyone's rules but his own.

Augusta glanced into his dark, turbulent eyes and knew she was way out of her league. She heard Garrison catch his breath as her small pink tongue moistened her suddenly dry lips. "I think it's time I said good night."

Garrison's hands clenched into fists of frustration as she slid by him and took a couple of steps. The need to taste her sweetness still pounded in his gut, but he'd be damned before he'd force himself on her. When he spoke, his voice was rough. "Sleep well, Gus."

She faltered at his use of her nickname. It had sounded like an endearment tumbling off his lips. "Good night, Garrison."

She hurried out of the tent without a backward glance. The entire camp was in darkness. They were the only ones up. She could make out her tent from the light spilling from the mess tent and the half moon. With a quick step and an eye out for any lost rattlers she unzipped her tent and hurried inside. After a moment of fumbling she located the lantern and lit it. She rapidly rezipped the tent before anything slithered in.

Secure in her own little world, she began to replay the scene with Garrison. How could she possibly be attracted to the guy? He was handsome, but she had known better-looking men and hadn't been instantly attracted to them. He was smart, even a genius when it came to dinosaurs, but that would be a repellent instead of an attraction. She avoided all geniuses. His charming personality needed some improvement, but considering the way she was thrust on him, she could hardly blame him for acting hostile. She reached for her buttons and began to undress.

Garrison extinguished the lantern in the mess hall with a curse. What did he think he was doing? In another minute he would have kissed her, lady or not. The gray sandstone grit must have clogged his brains. He knew the woman was going to be trouble since the day Old Bertram had interrupted his poker game. He just didn't think it would be this kind of trouble.

He left the dark tent and froze. The light from Augusta's lantern was casting her silhouette against her tent. She was undressing. He watched, mesmerized, as her blouse slipped down her arms. Her bra followed. He forgot to breathe. Firm, high breasts gently swayed as she wiggled out of her shorts. He knew it was his imagination, but he swore he could see the outline of each of her hardened nipples.

He resumed breathing when she slipped some type of shirt over her head and picked up a hairbrush. Her sweetly accented voice drifted on the light breeze as she counted the strokes she gave her hair. Garrison silently counted along with her to one hundred. Modern-day Gus was doing an amazingly old-fashioned custom. The lady had class.

She picked up something bulky and placed it on one end of the cot. He assumed it was a makeshift pillow. Regret and relief filled him as he watched her reach for the light and turn it off. Her tent was cloaked with blackness once again.

Garrison waited a few minutes before silently making his way to his tent. In the dark he undressed and slid into the sleeping bag. He felt like a peeping Tom. He felt hot and aroused. More important, he wondered how he was going to tell Augusta about undressing with the light on without embarrassing her, or himself.

Three

Augusta couldn't concentrate on her sketch of Glen and Randy, two of the male students, not with Harry recounting in blood-curdling detail the legend of the local Indian tribe who believed that the "terrible lizards" still roamed the earth. These dinosaurs were blamed for slaughtered cattle, vanishing sheep, and the occasional missing person.

Caroline threw a pebble at Harry's leg. "Shut up, Harry, you're scaring Augusta."

Augusta saw the victorious smile curving Harry's mouth. Stephen King would wear that grin upon learning one of his readers wouldn't turn off his light after finishing one of his books.

"Am I scaring you, Ms. Bodine?"

She shuddered at the way he pronounced her name. It was as though he knew her innermost thoughts and fears. "Don't you know any light-hearted tales that I could use in a children's book?" The other seven students were friendly and helpful, but not Harry. He seemed to resent her presence more than Garrison did.

"Did I tell you about the time the government held some nuclear testing and contaminated this entire area? I heard that every living thing was turned into hideous enormous mutants."

"Stop it, Harry," Ben snapped.

"A seventeen-foot rattler slithered into Hot Springs one afternoon, and his body was"—he held up his hands to form a huge circle—"this big around."

Augusta felt the pencil in her hand shake.

"Harry, if you don't shut your mouth, I'm going to do it for you." Ben's glare was mean enough to back up the threat.

Caroline and Stacy joined Augusta on her rock. "Don't listen to Harry. The government never did any testing around here, and there surely wasn't any nuclear fallout."

"Yeah, Harry's been reading too many of those strange comic books lately." Stacy looked at the drawing pad resting on Augusta's knees. "Wow! That's good."

Augusta gazed down at her preliminary sketch. It was okay, but it didn't deserve a *wow*. "Thanks. You guys don't mind if I use you as my models?"

"Heck no. If you do an extra sketch of me, could I have it to send to my mom?" Stacy asked.

Caroline cast Ben a wistful look and whispered, "If you do me, could you make me bigger in the chest department?"

Augusta smiled knowingly. "Sure." She looked

for Garrison but spotted only more gray sand-stone. "Isn't it about time we headed back?"

Ben studied the lowering sun and his watch. "Yeah, Augusta's right. Let's call it a day."

She packed her art supplies in her case, hoisted the nearly empty canteen and nylon tote bag, and joined the others for the walk back.

"Here, give me the case." Ben held out his hand.

"Thanks, but I'm used to carrying it." She glanced behind her once more. No sign of Garrison. He'd been avoiding her all day. He ate break-fast in the office and scowled at her during the entire hike to the site. He managed to stay and work with the students for an hour before heading off deeper into the Boneyard. He never returned for lunch, and if he didn't hurry, he was going to miss dinner.

Ben followed her gaze. "Doc's fine. He'll show up for dinner with either a backpack full of bones or a paper full of compass readings on our next excavating site."

"I wasn't worried." She forced herself to turn around and follow the group. "He's a strange man, isn't he?"

Ben chuckled. "I wouldn't use the word *strange* to describe Doc."

"What would you use?"

"The best. Doc Fisher is the best paleontologist on this continent."

"Are you sure, Ben?" she asked.

"If I weren't, I wouldn't be here."

Augusta squinted into the distance once more and wondered for the thousandth time that day if Garrison's kiss would be as good as his reputation on the field.

Garrison absently twirled a pencil in his hand as the students started to drift out of the mess tent for the night. He either had to tell Gus about her silhouetted striptease or he had to make sure no one else was wandering the camp when she performed it. The pencil stilled when she got up to leave. "Gus, may I have a word with you?"

She hesitated for a brief second. Her emotions weren't ready for another round like last night. "Sure." She walked over to the table he was at and sat down.

Garrison gazed at her bare arms and frowned. They were pink from too much sun, as were her legs and nose. "So how did your day go?"

Surprise flared in her eyes. She hadn't expected such a simple question. "It went real well. I got three great sketches of some of the students, and I helped to start uncover a femur."

His frown deepened. He had expected a complaint about the weather or living conditions. "Is there anything I could do to assist you?"

Lend me your Jeep so I can drive the sixty miles for a decent shower. Washing up out of a bucket or dipping into a two-foot-deep creek just didn't cut it. "Are the students always going to be working on the triceratops?"

"No, why?"

"I would like to sketch them doing different jobs on assorted fossils. Also, is there any chance that

I'll be able to follow you for a day or so to draw whatever it is a real paleontologist does?"

Garrison arched an eyebrow but refrained from commenting on exactly what he did all day. "I'm sure it could be arranged."

"Do you think the group from Princeton will allow me to tag along with them?"

"Why do you want to go with them?" His tone clearly indicated that he thought she would be wasting her time with them when she could have the best.

"I'm sure they do the same thing as you." She ignored his snort. "But they might do things a little differently, and I would like to note the variations in paleontologists' methods."

He didn't want her with the Ivy League team. They were color coordinated. Their backpacks matched their tents, sleeping bags, even their windbreakers. And they had a new deluxe, super-equipped four-wheel drive vehicle. He wasn't jealous of their material possessions; he had always been content with just having food on the table, a shirt on his back, and miles of dinosaurs' remains under his feet. But he had caught Sam Hoffman, the unmarried paleontologist, giving Augusta the once-over, and it had irked him. Just because Gus was off limits to him didn't mean she was available to every young, good-looking paleontologist who came along. "I'll see what I can arrange for you." That should keep her satisfied for days while he figured out another excuse.

"You're being awfully helpful all of a sudden."

"I resigned myself to my fate."

"Gee, thanks." She stood up to leave and yawned.

It was approaching eleven, and Garrison liked to start the day with the sun.

"You could have been a hell of a lot worse." She shot him a quizzical look. "Being new to camp life and all." She nodded in understanding. "As long as you obey the rules, things will work out just fine."

"In other words, obey you?"

"Well, I am in charge."

"Silly me. Here I thought we were actually going to have a pleasant conversation." She headed for the opening. "Good night, Doc, and don't let the dinosaurs bite."

Garrison smiled at the reappearance of her stubborn streak. "Good night, Gus," he called out as she disappeared into the blackness.

He waited a few minutes, then extinguished the lantern. He stood in the tent's opening, bracing a hand against a support pole, and stared at the darkened camp. Without turning around to look he knew Gus was undressing. Instincts and desires were burning a hole in his gut, but he refused to look. Instead, he studied the camp to make sure no one else was enjoying the show he had witnessed the previous night.

Her soft, gentle voice drifted out of the tent as she counted the brush strokes. Garrison felt every one of those strokes along his spine. Then a scream tore from her and she was tearing down the zipper of her tent, rushing outside right into his arms.

As his heart started to beat again, he asked, "What the hell?" He couldn't see anything in the darkness. He could only feel the violent shaking of her body. His arms closed protectively around her.

Hastily lit lanterns, running feet, and voices filled the night behind him.

"What's wrong?"

Garrison turned to Ben and Randy, the first two students to reach him. "Check her tent, but be careful."

Ben and Randy cautiously approached the tent, half expecting to meet a rattler. Ben sighed with relief when he didn't spot one and entered the tent. Immediately he saw an eight-inch lizard standing frozen on the ground. He chuckled. Augusta's scream scared the poor thing more than it had scared her. He reached for the culprit, but his hand halted in midair. The little lizard was standing by the lantern, most likely attracted to the warmth, and it cast an eight-foot shadow. No wonder Augusta screamed; the thing gave him the creeps after listening to Harry's horror stories all day.

"What is it?" Garrison demanded. He felt helpless just standing there, but with a hundred-and-ten-pound woman plastered to his chest, there wasn't much else he could do. Turning Gus over to someone else was unthinkable.

Ben picked up the little fellow and left the tent. "See, Augusta, this was all it was."

Garrison felt her arms tighten around his neck and frowned. Something wasn't right. Augusta didn't seem the type to panic over a little lizard. He pinned Ben with a look. He wanted a further explanation.

Ben shot a quick glance at Harry standing at the

back of the crowd. "The little fellow was standing by her lantern, casting a huge, monstrous shadow on the back wall of her tent. If I'd spotted the shadow instead of the lizard first, I would have joined Augusta in your arms."

Augusta finally raised her head and stared at the little fellow. "Lord, he fits in your hand."

Garrison tightened his hold as Augusta tried to disengage herself from his arms. She felt too good, all soft and womanly snuggled up against his chest. The swell of her unbound breasts was pressing into his shirt, causing his hormones to shift into high gear. His fantasy of last night was in his arms, and he wasn't ready to let go.

Augusta reached out and tapped the lizard on the nose. "You shouldn't sneak up on someone like that. I almost had heart failure."

Ben chuckled and placed the lizard on the ground. In a flash of scurrying legs he disappeared between two tents and into the night. "I'm afraid the zipper on your tent is shot. It's going to have to be replaced."

"I'll handle it," Garrison said firmly. "The party's over. Everyone head on back to your tents and get some sleep."

The students and the paleontologists from Princeton gave Garrison and Augusta a few curious looks before doing as told.

Augusta frowned. "You can release me now."

Garrison gazed up at the stars and started to count them. He couldn't have released her in front of the students because of his condition. His hormones had overruled his common sense and they had caused a very masculine reaction to her nearness.

"Garrison?" Augusta's voice was uneven.

His hands clutched at the silkiness of her nightshirt as he kept her glued to his body and marched over to his tent. He unfastened the zipper and stepped into the darkness with her.

"Garrison, what are—"

His mouth stole the remaining words.

Her surprise was quickly overtaken by desire. Red-hot swirling desire curled its way along her every nerve ending. She answered his demanding mouth with a primitive need of her own.

Garrison met the sweet dance of her tongue as he cupped her silk-clad bottom and brought her in intimate contact with his pulsing arousal. A moan shook his chest as her creamy thighs parted. His feet took two faulty steps toward his cot, when the realization of who he was kissing hit him. Augusta was a lady who rated more than a quick toss on his cot. She deserved romance, love, and happily-ever-after. Everything he couldn't give her.

Augusta tightened her hold on his shoulders as he broke the kiss. It hadn't been enough. She wanted more.

"I shouldn't have done that."

She wished it weren't so dark in there. She wanted to see the expression on his face. He was telling her one thing, but his body was saying another. "Why? Because I'm Bertram's granddaughter?"

He broke the physical contact, located a flashlight, and picked out his cot and sleeping bag. "I don't give a damn about Bertram. Every woman I've ever kissed was somebody's granddaughter."

Augusta blinked as her desire continued to swirl out of control. "Then why?"

Her face looked pale and fragile in the dim light. He felt an overwhelming urge to wrap her in his arms. But instead he gathered up the sleeping bag and thrust the flashlight in her hand. "I'm the one who has to look in the mirror tomorrow morning." He walked out of the tent. "I'll be right back."

What in the hell was that supposed to mean? Didn't everyone look at themselves in a mirror in the morning?

Garrison returned with her sleeping bag and the rolled-up sweatshirt she was using as a pillow. Tossing them onto his cot, he said, "Get some sleep. The kids are heading for a new location first thing in the morning."

"It's really not necessary to switch tents with me tonight. I can assure you, my imagination is under control now."

"It wouldn't be safe for you with the zipper broken. Anything could slip in during the night."

The way he phrased the warning caused her to smile. She didn't think he was referring to cute lizards or deadly rattlers. It had more to do with a two-legged animal. "What about you?"

"I'm a big boy. I can take care of myself."

"And I can't?" A blush swept up her cheeks as she remembered dashing from her tent and waking the entire camp all because of a harmless reptile.

He didn't respond to the question. Instead, he

merely said, "Good night, Gus," went out, and rezipped the flaps. The silhouette of her prehistoric beast might have frightened her, but it was nothing compared to the fear he had been experiencing since gazing at her silhouette the night before. He wanted Augusta as he had no other woman, but he was paralyzed with the fear that once he had her, he wouldn't be able to let her go. There wasn't room in his life for a woman who was used to all the finer things in life. Hadn't Catherine already proved that point? With a heavy step he slowly made his way to her tent and another sleepless night.

August fluffed up her sweatshirt and tried to settle down. She couldn't. Garrison's rejection had confused her and his presence was too strong in the tent. His duffel bag sat in the corner overflowing with clothes, while in the other corner was a crate with his shaving mug and toothbrush. A folding table was weighted down with papers, books, bones, and assorted paraphernalia. Everywhere she looked, she saw him.

She snuggled down into the sleeping bag, thankful that at least he hadn't humiliated her by bursting out laughing over her reaction to the lizard. Remembering the lizard brought a very important question to her mind. How did the lizard get into her zipped-up-tight tent?

Early the following morning, Garrison was on his way to breakfast when he heard Augusta's voice drifting from behind the empty mess tent.

He stopped in his tracks to listen. "I want to know why you did it, Harry."

"Who said I did anything?"

"I know you put the lizard in my tent last night. I want to know why."

Garrison kept still and quiet. He wanted to know what else was happening in his camp he hadn't been aware of.

"You don't belong here. No one wants you here."

Garrison was taken aback by the hatred vibrating in Harry's voice. He had heard enough. He was halfway around the tent when Augusta's reply stopped him.

"I know, Harry." There was a moment's pause. "I'm not trying to be one of the students or run the show. I need to be here. It's my job. How could I do a book on paleontologists and dinosaurs without being here?"

"You used the fact that your grandfather is the dean to blackmail Dr. Fisher into allowing you to come." Garrison could easily imagine Harry sneering as he threw that accusation.

"How did you know I was the dean's granddaughter?"

"I heard Doc having it out with Dr. Newman weeks ago."

"You shouldn't have listened to other people's arguments, Harry. You might not get the true picture. My grandfather is totally against my being here."

"He is?"

"Yes. I went behind his back and wrote to Dr. Newman for permission. Dr. Newman never connected my last name of Bodine to Grandfather's Fremont. Authorization was granted before either my grandfather or Dr. Fisher knew of the letter."

"Then you did trick Dr. Fisher?"

"No. Dr. Fisher should have been at the staff meeting. I didn't realize he hadn't approved my visit until I got here." There was another brief pause. "I still would have come though. This trip is too important to me. Garrison has accepted my presence, why can't you?"

"He has?"

"If you don't believe me, why don't you ask him?"

"Are you going to tell him about the lizard?" Harry didn't sound so sure of himself anymore.

"Are you going to try another stunt like that to scare me away?"

"No."

"Then I don't see any reason Garrison has to know, do you?"

"Uh, no." There was a hint of respect in Harry's voice. "Thanks, Ms. Bodine."

"Call me Augusta. Everyone else does."

"Can I say one more thing, Augusta?"

"Of course."

"You sure do have a set of lungs on you. You nearly gave me a heart attack. I thought something really awful was happening to you."

Augusta chuckled as Harry walked away.

Garrison quietly made his way back to the center of the camp. He didn't want Augusta to know he had overheard her conversation with Harry. She had handled herself well and he was disappointed that he couldn't ride to her rescue again. In his frustrated state he would have kicked Harry out of the Boneyard without waiting for any explanations. Garrison had better savor his having acted the knight in shining armor because Gus didn't seem as though she would need a lot of rescuing in the future.

Four

Garrison assembled the group, placed Ben in charge, and handed him the coordinates for the new dig site. The area he had marked off the day before had felt hot under his feet. He knew there was something spectacular buried beneath the sandstone.

"Aren't you coming with us?" Randy asked.

"No, I have a couple of things to do in town this morning. I'll see you back in camp around dinner-time." He watched as the group headed out, with Augusta sandwiched in the middle, dressed in a T-shirt and shorts and clunky hiking boots. On her head was the battered baseball cap he'd given her the first day. His lips twitched at the picture she made, carrying her briefcase into the barren landscape. She should have looked ridiculous instead of so lovable.

• • •

Augusta wiped her perspiring forehead with a handkerchief. It had to be ninety-five degrees even though it was early evening. They were coming in sight of the camp, and even the prospect of wading in a murky creek in her bathing suit sounded like heaven.

"What the hell is that?"

Augusta looked up to see what Randy was referring to. Next to the mess tent, where her tent had stood that morning, was a huge hunk of metal with a door. It looked like a battered UFO.

They cautiously made their way forward. The block of metal had four wheels, one of which was flat, causing the thing to lean drunkenly. The windows were half glass and half torn plastic. She looked at the rest of the group and wondered if she was wearing the same dazed expression they were. Her voice was barely above a whisper, when she asked, "Is it a camper?"

Everyone jumped as a loud thud came from the interior, followed by a muttered curse. Either it was haunted, or someone was in there.

Ben looked at Augusta for some guidance. She shrugged her shoulders. He squared his and pounded on the bent aluminum screen door. "Hey, you in there, come out!"

The door was thrown open with such force, the lower hinge snapped off. Garrison jumped the two and a half feet to the ground, avoiding using the metal step that was dangling by a bolt. "Oh, good, you're back." He gestured at the camper and beamed. "Isn't she a beauty?"

The man was positively glowing when he turned to Augusta and asked, "Well, what do you think?"

Augusta squeaked, "Me?"

"Well, since it's going to be your home for the next six weeks, yours is the only opinion that matters."

Augusta felt every eye in camp on her. She wanted to cry, plead, and beg for this not to be happening. Garrison had wanted to scare her off with tales of rattlers and wild passion and failed. She was afraid he had just found his target. She would rather sleep on the ground with the snakes than step one foot into that overgrown dog food can. She mustered the best smile she could and stammered, "It's interesting."

Garrison tilted his head. "Interesting?"

Augusta looked pleadingly at the students. She was in dire need of help. When none was forthcoming, she managed a weak smile. "Where did it come from?"

He scratched his head as he continued to study the camper. "I borrowed it from Lucky Hawk."

"Who's Lucky Hawk?"

"He owns the gas station in town. I traded him a couple of bones for the rent."

"You gave him *real* dinosaur bones for this?"

"They weren't museum quality. Even the university couldn't use them. Lucky Hawk knows that, but he could still make a nice bundle from some tourists." Garrison held open the tilting door. "Come on. I'll give you the five-cent tour. It has all the comforts of home."

Augusta glared murderously at the retreating backs of the students as they slunk away. With a weary sigh she hauled herself up to the doorway.

Garrison groaned as her sweet tush reached eye

level. A sheen of perspiration glistened on the backs of her seductive thighs. A man could make his last meal of those thighs and die happy. *Maybe this wasn't such a good idea.* He had persuaded Lucky Hawk to lend him the camper because the thought of Gus undressing in her lighted tent that night was more than his hormones could stand.

She glanced curiously around the camper and wrinkled her nose as the smell of ammonia assaulted her. "Did you say something?"

Garrison pulled himself up and joined her in the cramped kitchen. "I said, I will have to find you a step."

Augusta trembled slightly at his nearness. There was probably no more than nine square feet of floor space in the camper, and Garrison's presence left her no room to move unless she brushed up against him. Something she was trying to avoid.

The kitchen consisted of a ten-inch sink, a two-burner stove, eight inches of counter space, and a refrigerator the size of a shoebox crammed against one wall. On the opposite wall were two cabinets above a cushioned bench and a two-foot-square Formica table. Everything looked well used but gleamed with a recent cleaning. Hence, the overpowering ammonia smell.

"Did you see the bedroom?"

Augusta stared at Garrison's eyes. The pupils weren't dilated, so he couldn't be using any hallucinogenics. The man was serious. Where would a bedroom fit? Her glance followed his outstretched arm and she spotted a mattress at the far end of the camper. With a hesitant step she squeezed into the twenty-inch hall. Sure enough, there was a bed. Her duffel bag and an unfamiliar huge carryall were placed in the center of the mattress, which was sitting on warped wooden drawers that opened into the hallway. More cabinets hung from the low ceiling above it. Windows surrounded the bed on three sides. She would have to crawl into bed every night or risk physical damage to her body.

She turned to Garrison, who was beaming again. "I've saved the best for last," he said.

"There's more?"

With a flourish Garrison opened a door in the hallway, blocking her against the mattress. "Oh, sorry." He closed the door so she could step into the kitchen, and then reopened it.

The way Garrison was acting, Augusta half expected to find a ballroom complete with a twelve-piece orchestra. It was probably a closet. Keeping the smile plastered on her face, she peered inside. A soft gasp escaped her lips. "It's a bathroom!" The tiny green cubicle with a small commode, sink, and mirror could have been a rest room on an airplane, but like the rest of the camper, it was impeccably clean.

She stepped into the small space and hesitantly turned the faucet. Cool, clean water poured into the basin and trickled through her fingers. Tears filled her eyes. She had running water. Garrison was a magician.

"You've missed the best part."

Augusta turned off the water and raised her eyes to gaze at the man filling the doorway. Scratch the magician part, he was a god. Her voice held awe as once again she asked, "There's more?"

With a grin he reached into the room, took a hand-held shower hose from its hook on the wall, and gave it to her. He pointed it toward the side wall and turned on the spigot.

Augusta came out of her daze as cold water ricocheted off the wall and started to soak her. With a squeal of delight she looked at the shower head and then at Garrison. "It's a shower!"

At that moment Garrison knew that every ounce of trouble he had gone through to get the camper had been worth it. Towing the camper the last three miles with a flat tire now seemed trivial. Gus loved the camper, or, more accurately, she loved the bathroom. He started to laugh in triumph, but then he encountered her gaze. Emotions blazed there, and they weren't gratitude.

Augusta swallowed hard as everything in the world disappeared but the man standing in front of her. He had just handed her the most precious gift she had ever received in her life. He had known, without being told, how important something as ordinary as a shower was to her. A diamond tiara wouldn't have done her any good in the Boneyard, but a shower meant comfort. And if he was worried about her comfort, he must want her to stay. The kiss had meant something to him, and mirrors be damned!

"Don't look at me like that," Garrison growled.

"Like what?"

His intense glance traveled up tanned legs, taking in every drop of water slowly making their way over every curve. Her denim shorts were spotted with moisture, and the pale blue T-shirt was soaked and clinging to her breasts. Desire pounded through his body, and his hands gripped the doorjamb as he forced his gaze upward. He eyed the delicate pulse that was beating madly under the creamy smoothness of her neck. Garrison's breath lodged in his throat as the tip of her tongue slowly came out and moistened her lower lip. His gaze quickly shot up to her golden eyes and the heat there. "Like you need to kiss me as much as I need to taste you again."

Augusta held his probing gaze and remained silent.

Garrison tightened his grip on the wooden frame. The lady was becoming too tempting. He swallowed hard and asked for something he was positive she wouldn't give. "You're going to have to tell me what you want." He never forced himself on an unwilling female, and if she wasn't going to admit the attraction, she was unwilling.

Augusta was oblivious to the cool water still splattering her clothes and heated skin. Garrison was waiting for her to give permission before he kissed her. Did she somehow give him the wrong impression the other night when he kissed her? Impossible! At least now she would have the light of day to read his expression. Her voice breathless with anticipation, she said, "I want you to kiss me."

He froze for a heartbeat. His surprise was overshadowed by one fierce raw emotion—desire. Primitive urges swelled, and every muscle throughout his body quivered with need as he stepped into the cubicle and hauled her into his arms.

Augusta answered the demand of his mouth and parted her lips to deepen the kiss. Wicked and sinfully delicious sensations emerged from every fiber of her being. This was a man who knew how to kiss, and she wanted it to go on forever. With a moan of pleasure she wrapped her arms around his neck.

Garrison's roar filled the small bathroom as cold water soaked him.

Augusta stepped back and flattened herself against the wall. Her stunned gaze went from Garrison to the flowing shower head still clutched in her hand.

"Is this your way of telling me to take a cold shower?" He softly chuckled as he reached for the faucet and turned the water off. He pulled the front of his T-shirt out of his jeans and tried to dry his face, which had taken the spray when Gus jumped back.

Augusta's golden gaze was riveted to Garrison's exposed stomach. Firm muscles rippled like the smooth surface of a pond after a pebble had been thrown in. An intriguing patch of dark curls started below his navel and disappeared into the low waistband of his jeans. She slowly placed the shower hose back onto its hook and flattened her palms against the cool wall behind her before she gave in to the temptation to stroke each fascinating ripple.

Garrison lowered the shirt, glanced at Gus, and took a deep breath. It was no use. The cool water hadn't diminished his desire. He still needed Gus with a burning intensity that went beyond lust. The need to taste her sweetness was as vital as his next breath. He stepped closer and tenderly cupped her cheek. "Do you have any idea what you are doing to me?"

She leaned into the warmth of his palm. "Probably the same thing you are doing to me."

His thumb stroked the pink moistness of her lower lip. He felt her soft sigh feather his thumb and shuddered. "I still don't think this is such a good idea."

"You said that before."

He brushed a gentle kiss where his thumb had been a heartbeat before. "You don't believe me?"

The graceful and refined fingers of an artist reached up and caressed his stubble-covered jaw. "I'll believe in the Easter bunny, Santa Claus, and the existence of aliens before I'll believe you won't kiss me again."

Garrison's chuckle was low and rough. "Always knew you were smart." He bent his head and lovingly took her mouth. He couldn't allow a mature, gorgeous woman to go around believing in the Easter bunny, now, could he?

The kiss started slowly, sweet, and hot. Augusta stretched up on her toes, tangled her fingers into his dark hair, and pulled him closer. Heat flooded her body, dissolving the existing reality that surrounded them. There was only Garrison, heat, and this moment.

A shiver slid down Garrison's back as soft, damp, and rounded breasts pressed against his chest. The fragile grip he exerted on his control was in grave danger of slipping. Rapidly.

He released the succulent sweetness of her mouth and trailed his lips down her jaw to the satiny smoothness of her throat. His harsh groan of need was muttered against the throbbing pulse.

Augusta arched her neck to allow Garrison better access. Heat from his hands simmered through her wet shirt as he tenderly gripped her waist and lifted her up against the wall. A feverish blaze erupted deep inside her. His lips captured one of her wet, protruding nipples through the soaked shirt. Her fingers tightened in his hair as she tried to pull him closer. It was impossible. He would have to be inside her to be any closer. She could feel the trembling of his muscles, his heat sizzling between their wet clothes, and the hard shaft of his desire pressing against the womanly softness at the cradle of her thighs. The desire pulsating there was echoed by the liquid heat raging from her abdomen and gathering at the junction of her need. She wanted Garrison Fisher more than she wanted her next breath.

Garrison pulled the tight bud deeper into his mouth and ignored the pounding in his head.

"Doc . . . Augusta . . . dinner is ready."

His instantaneous release of Gus as Randy's voice drifted into the camper caused her to falter for a second on the slippery floor. The pounding hadn't been in his head, it had been one of his students banging on the door. What in the world had he been thinking? He had been on the brink of making love to Gus in a three-by-three bathroom within ten yards of his students. Thankfully someone had stepped in with a timely interruption. What he needed now was another cold shower and his head examined. The worst thing he could have done was to fall deeper under Gus's tempting spell. The lady had to be part witch.

With a moan of frustration and relief he ran his hand through his damp hair and raised his voice. "We'll be right there."

Augusta silently watched the play of emotions across Garrison's face. She couldn't tell if he was relieved, angry, or frustrated. She knew she was feeling all three. Relief that Randy just didn't walk in, anger because he interrupted them, and frustration because Garrison seemed to be backing off again.

Garrison glanced at the front of Gus's T-shirt and swallowed hard. Twin peaks were puckering the wet material, begging for his attention. With his last ounce of control he stepped out of the bathroom and into the safer kitchen. "Take a shower and change before coming to the mess tent." He turned toward the bent screen door as she stepped into the hallway.

"Garrison?"

He had the door open and his retreat almost complete when her provocative southern drawl reached him. Against his better judgment he slowly looked over his shoulder.

Augusta slowly smiled. His seemingly careless withdrawal was more like a desperate escape. "Thank you for the shower."

His hungry gaze went from her kiss-swollen lips to the pleading nipples. With a muttered curse that didn't sound like *you're welcome,* he slammed out of the camper.

• • •

Twenty-five minutes later Augusta was in the mess tent helping herself to a bowl of canned stew and a hard roll. Sunday was only two days away, and the promised trip into town was beginning to sound like paradise. Her first stop was going to be the diner the students kept telling her about and the biggest stack of pancakes she could eat. But for tonight she'd eat anything put in front of her. She was famished, squeaky clean, and secretly delighted.

After Garrison had stormed out of the camper she had gone to see what was in the other bag on the bed. Her surprise had turned into delight as she pulled out an unopened package of peach-colored sheets, a matching blanket, and a down-filled pillow. Garrison had not only wanted her to live in comfort, but to sleep in it too. The man was sending out so many conflicting signals that if he were a lighthouse, she'd be washed up on the rocks by now. He kissed her to the fringe of ecstasy and then stormed out. He told her he wanted her to leave and then he borrowed a camper and bought her fancy sheets. *He either wants to drive me crazy or take me to bed.*

She glanced across the mess tent. Garrison and the paleontologists from Princeton were in a heated debate about the theory that a huge comet wiped out the dinosaurs at the end of the Cretaceous period. In the middle of a sentence Garrison turned and looked directly at her. One prayer slammed into her mind. *Please let him take me to bed.*

"What took you so long, Augusta?"

She turned away from Garrison's probing gaze and looked at Caroline. "I was taking a shower."

Caroline's mouth dropped open for a full minute before she yelled, "A shower?"

Augusta chuckled as a look of total envy crossed the young woman's face. How could she possibly enjoy her good fortune and Garrison's generosity without sharing it? "Why don't you go take one yourself?"

Caroline jumped to her feet and looked ready to kiss her before dashing out of the mess tent. Her parting *Thanks* echoed in the unusually quiet tent. Augusta looked around and encountered ten pairs of envious eyes and one pair of hostile brown ones, Garrison's. She felt like the dog holding the juicy bone being surrounded by a pack of starving wolves. "You all may take turns using it. I certainly don't own it."

"Really?"

"Neat!"

"I'm next."

Augusta relaxed. They weren't going to rip her apart for the bone. "Just remember the water's one temperature—cold—and there's no electricity in the camper, so it can be used only in daylight."

"You seem to be forgetting one thing." Garrison's voice rumbled across the distance.

"What?"

"Water."

Augusta blinked. What was he talking about? Of course they weren't forgetting about the water, it's the single most important element to a shower. "What about it?"

"Where do you think all that clean cold water is coming from?"

She was stopped short by the lack of an answer. Where was all the water coming from anyway? "I don't know."

"I filled the camper's holding tanks from our water truck. If it was just Gus taking a shower, we wouldn't miss the water, but since everyone wants one, the water truck will have to be refilled every week."

Groans echoed throughout the tent. Not understanding the problem, Augusta shrugged her shoulders and said, "So?"

Ben took pity on her. "The water truck has been around since the Second World War. So has its shocks, tires, and oil-burning engine. The thing is an environmental disaster waiting to happen, but the university doesn't count replacing a water truck as a high priority. Driving the forty miles into Hot Springs three times a summer is one thing, but every week would be pushing it beyond its limits."

"Who usually drives it?"

"Doc does." With a laugh Ben added, "He's the only one who knows enough curses to keep it going for the eighty-mile round trip."

Augusta looked at Garrison, who had been silent throughout the exchange. "Can it make the trip weekly?"

"I'm a paleontologist, not a magician. Besides, I don't think that many curses have been invented yet."

Augusta bit her lip. It was a nice gesture on Garrison's part, but if the rest of the crew couldn't use the shower, neither could she.

Sam Hoffman, the young paleontologist from Princeton, spoke up. "I'm willing to drive the truck in this weekend. I'm sure I could think up some inventive names to call it."

Barry Elison, the other paleontologist, said, "I'll take it next weekend, but my wife, Sue, will have to do the hollering and name-calling. If anyone could intimidate a truck, Sue can."

Ben, Randy, and Steve, another student, quickly added their willingness to try. Everyone looked at Garrison and waited for his decision.

Garrison studied the set of Gus's jaw. The southern peach had a pit, and it was called stubbornness. He could tell from the angle of her chin she wouldn't be using the shower again if no one else was allowed access to it. He wouldn't put it past her if she pitched her broken tent out in the middle of camp just to prove her point. With a weary sigh of defeat he gave in. "All right, if everyone pitches in on the driving and the maintenance of the truck." The cheer that went up vibrated the canvas walls of the tent. "But there are some conditions attached to it."

The room suddenly turned quiet. "The camper is for Augusta's personal use, and it's only because of her good graces everyone is allowed the use of the shower. It is to be treated as her home, and her privacy shall be observed at all times. Second, since there are thirteen of us living here, and the water truck won't be able to handle ninety-one showers a week *and* our water needs, the showers are rationed at one every other night per person."

"Fine."

"No problem."

Garrison stood up and headed out of the tent before Augusta could voice her thanks.

Augusta stood in the gathering dusk and silently watched Garrison as he waded through a mountain of papers spread across a makeshift desk in the office. His hair had fallen across his brow, giving him a boyish appearance, and his mouth was pulled into a frown of concentration. He looked like a little boy struggling with his homework. Her watchful artist's gaze memorized every detail of his expression.

Garrison slowly lifted his eyes and squinted against the glare of the lantern. Someone was standing outside the tent, watching him, and he had a feeling deep in his gut it was the one person he was trying to avoid, Gus. He had barely hung on to his control through dinner. Having her within the same tent would be pushing him to the limit.

She knew the instant he spotted her. With a small smile she entered the tent. "I hope I'm not disturbing you."

You disturb me more than you'd ever know. "No, I'm just finishing up here. Is there something I can do for you?"

Oh, merciful heavens, yes! "No. I just wanted to thank you for all you've done. The camper is a godsend, especially the shower." Her small coral-tipped nail lightly ran down the length of a bone being used as a paperweight. "Everyone agreed that the women could use the shower tonight and tomorrow night it's the men's turn."

His eyes followed the small, sexy fingernail. Who would have thought the sight of a coral-tipped nail would increase his blood pressure? "That—" He cleared the roughness from his throat and started again. "That sounds fair."

"They wanted me to tell you that you have first dibs on the shower tomorrow night."

Standing naked in her shower held some appealing possibilities. Maybe he should stick to bathing in the creek until his libido returned to normal. "If I'm in from the field early, I'll take them up on their offer. If not, I'll wait my turn just like everyone else."

She tried to see if memories of what had happened in the shower hours before were revealed in his eyes. The only thing she could detect was the reflection of the lantern's glow. The encounter had to have meant something to him. It couldn't have been all one-sided. "How much do I owe you for the sheets and blanket?"

The reflection gleaming in his eyes seemed to have gotten a shade brighter. "Nothing. I'll figure out a way to claim it on my expense account."

"The university's accounting department will have a field day knowing you purchased peach-colored sheets."

A grin curved his lips. "It won't be the first, or I'm sure the last, time they enjoyed some of my *questionable* purchases."

Augusta frowned. She didn't want to hear about his past encounters or what he bought then. She cared only about the here and now. "How did you know I like to sleep with a pillow?"

Visions of her silhouette rolling up a sweatshirt and placing it at the head of her cot flashed through his mind. "You had a bunched-up shirt at the top of your sleeping bag the night I switched tents with you."

Stop being so diplomatic and polite. "Oh, you mean the night I acted like an idiot over a lizard?"

"It was a perfectly understandable reaction given the situation."

Augusta looked around the tent for something to hit him over the head with. The man was purposely being dense and distant. She had deliberately tracked him down while the students were busy playing poker in the mess tent. She hadn't been in the mood for card games, and she surely wasn't in the mood for whatever game Garrison was playing. When she had entered the tent, she had been half hoping they'd pick up where they left off, or at least be on more friendly terms. Obviously, Garrison had other ideas on the subject. She eyed the massive bone lying under a worktable and wondered how heavy it was. "I noticed a crate had been placed where the step should have been on the camper. I gather I owe you another thanks."

Garrison forced his hands and the rest of his body to remain steady as sweat dripped down his back. The tent's temperature had risen twenty degrees since Gus had stepped inside. She was noticeably edgy about something. What did she think he was going to do, pounce on her? He had learned his lesson that afternoon. He couldn't get within five feet of her without having to kiss her. And once he kissed her, *wham!* spontaneous combustion. It would take a January dig in Glacier National Park to cool him down. "No thanks necessary. It's a long way to a hospital from out here."

Frustrated, she asked point-blank, "Why exactly did you go through all the trouble of getting me the camper?"

"It's safer for you in a camper than in a tent."

"And?"

Sweat broke out across his brow. "I presumed you needed space for your paints, papers, or whatever else you artist types use."

"And?"

The paper clutched in his fist tore. "You're a lady, and ladies don't go around slumming in sleeping bags or have scaly green night visitors."

"Thank you for thinking I'm a lady. But I still don't see what the difference between me and the other females in the camp is. They all sleep in sleeping bags."

"They aren't *ladies*," Garrison roared. "They're paleontologists, or at least training to be."

Augusta chuckled. "Are you telling me that if you thought they were ladies, they wouldn't be here?"

"Damn straight. The Boneyard is no place for a lady."

"That's why you want me out of here. Because I'm a lady, not because I'm a children's writer and illustrator. It's because I'm female." Disappointment cracked in her voice. How could she have misjudged him so?

"There's a difference between being a female and being a lady."

Her chin rose an inch. "How did I get the illustrious title of *lady* instead of female?"

Garrison stood up and ran his fingers through his tousled hair. "I'll start with the prim business suit and the matching shoes. Look at you now, your hair is shiny clean and I can detect the subtle fragrance of expensive perfume. I'll bet there isn't one ounce of dirt underneath those perfectly manicured fingernails."

She glared across the tent and refused to look at her nails. She had just spent the last half hour in the mess tent fixing the damage the past two days had done to them. "I won't apologize for my personal hygiene or my taste in clothes. If that makes me a *lady* in your eyes, so be it. I'm damn proud to be a lady." She stepped closer to his worktable and shook her finger at him. "I'll prove to you that a *lady* can survive in the Boneyard if it's the last thing I do."

At that instant Garrison believed her. "Does that mean you will be giving up that nice soft mattress and clean sheets?"

"Hell no. Do I look stupid to you?" She turned on her heel and headed out of the tent. The man was impossible. She'd show him exactly what kind of lady she was.

No, Gus, you don't look stupid. You look gorgeous, classy, and entirely too sexy for my peace of mind. With a weary frustrated sigh Garrison sat down and glared around the empty tent. He hadn't meant to challenge her. Wasn't the South known for its muleheadedness? Half the population of Georgia still thought they should have won the Civil War. The faint tantalizing fragrance Gus had been wearing lingered in the air. Damn if he couldn't smell magnolia blossoms.

Five

Garrison turned off the faucet, cracked open the bathroom door, and reached for his towel, hanging on a hook in the hallway. He buried his face in the soft terry-cloth as Augusta's sweet voice drifted in through the windows of the camper. She was still sitting out front, enjoying the cool evening with Sam Hoffman. With a few vicious swipes of the towel Garrison finished drying himself and stepped out into the hallway to retrieve his clean clothes. It was time to send Sammy packing.

After Gus had stormed out of the office last night Garrison had retired to his tent to spend the remainder of the night in misery. Gus had been wrong. Ladies and the Boneyard wouldn't mix; their main ingredients violently contradicted each other. So why was he so frustrated? He knew the outcome before the results were in. When he was eight years old he had found his first fossil, and dinosaur fever had gotten into his blood. His next twenty-eight years were driven by that raging fever. It still controlled him today. If dinosaurs roamed the earth for one hundred and forty million years, surely it was going to take more than his lifetime to understand them. The fever was a commitment. For nine months out of the year he taught and encouraged young men and women who would be the future paleontologists. By sharing his knowledge he was giving them that extra step forward. The remaining three months were spent doing what he loved best, finding the evidence to back up his theories on how the magnificent beasts had lived. The hard-core physical proof came only one way, with backbreaking work, long hours, and sacrifices. He had accepted those sacrifices years before. So why was he beginning to feel life was cheating him?

Garrison straightened up the bathroom—the one disadvantage of being last to use the shower—gathered up his dirty clothes, and stepped outside.

"Honestly, Augusta, I would love the company on the harrowing drive into Hot Springs tomorrow." Sam Hoffman turned toward Garrison, who was stepping out of the camper, a frown on his face.

"Thank you, Sam, it's really sweet of you to ask." Augusta had heard Garrison come up behind her but refused to acknowledge his presence. She was still a little peeved at him for his behavior the night before.

"But she can't accept your offer," Garrison interrupted.

Augusta turned in her canvas deck chair and

glared at Garrison, standing behind her. "I beg your pardon?"

"I said, you won't be able to accompany Sam into town tomorrow."

"Why not?"

"Because you will be riding in with me."

Augusta arched one delicate eyebrow. "I will?"

Sam rose and gazed curiously at Augusta, then at Garrison. The tension sizzling between them could generate enough electricity to supply the entire state of Montana. Whatever was happening was definitely on a personal level, and he knew a third wheel when he was rolled into one. "Well, since that's settled, I guess I'll be going." He smiled reassuringly at Augusta. "If you change your mind, I'll be leaving at about eight o'clock."

Augusta watched Sam walk away and forced a smile when she really felt like screaming and throwing something. The dominating male stated his intentions and the less aggressive male was backing down. Well, dammit, she wasn't some available female looking for a mate. All she wanted was a ride into town.

Garrison mentally braced himself for a fight as he casually sat in the chair Sam had just vacated. By the ferocious gleam in Gus's eye he knew he was about to be blasted with both barrels. He didn't want to fight with her, but there was no way he was allowing her to ride into Hot Springs with Mr. Yuppie. Still he flinched at the callous way he had handled the situation.

Augusta was just about to open her mouth and let him have it when she noticed the flinch. Garrison didn't feel as cool as he was acting, she concluded. He was expecting a fight, and, by hell, just because he was expecting a battle, she wasn't going to give him one. She was tired of being the only one thrown off balance by this attraction between them. She forced her face into a polite mask and purred, "That's awful sweet of you to ask, Garrison."

His mouth opened to rebut the first shot. "I—" He slammed it shut as soon as her words sank in.

She hid her secret delight. "What time will you be ready to leave?"

Dazed, he said, "If we leave by seven, we could have breakfast in Hot Springs."

"Wonderful! I've been dreaming of pancakes for days." Deciding that a hasty retreat was needed, she stood up. "My, look at the time. I have some finishing touches to be put on some of my drawings." She took a step toward the camper door. "I'll see you around seven." She opened the screen door. "Oh, and Garrison?"

He stood up and frowned. "Yeah?"

"Thanks again." Augusta stepped up into the camper and closed the screen door behind her. She bit her lip to keep from laughing out loud as she watched Garrison mutter something and slowly walk away, shaking his head. She lightly licked her index finger and drew an imaginary "1" in the air. Her grin stretched from ear to ear as she whispered, "Strike one for the lady."

Garrison jammed the Jeep into second gear and shot another quick glance at the woman sitting next to him. He had spent half the night tossing and turning, trying to figure out what she was up to. The answer the sleepless night had brought was the same as it was before he had entered his tent. A big fat zero. He had no idea what had possessed her to meekly agree to accompany him into town. The Gus he was beginning to know and admire hadn't a meek bone in her body.

The morning sun lightly caressed Augusta's face as she leaned her head back against the Jeep's seat and tilted up her face. Lord, Montana was a beautiful state. She ignored the questioning glances Garrison had been sending her way since she met him by the Jeep. It served him right if he was perplexed. Nobody could be more bewildered than she. When Garrison had walked away mumbling into the evening, she had debated riding into town with the students or Sam, and letting "Mr. God's Gift to the Dinosaurs" stew for the day. But something stopped her. She wanted to be with Garrison. The students and crew were nice, polite, and friendly toward her, but it was Garrison who fascinated her. The man was a mass of conflicting signals and instant attraction. She would bet her favorite watercolors that the attraction was mutual. So why was he fighting it?

The treacherous ride into Hot Springs was done in silence. Augusta hung on and worshiped the sun while Garrison concentrated on the road. She straightened up as they reached the edge of town and studied Hot Springs more closely. It was a typical small town stuck in the middle of nowhere. Everything was on one main street that cut through the center of town. A smile came to her lips as she viewed the small array of stores waiting for her to discover.

Garrison pulled the Jeep into a parking space and turned off the engine. "We've made it."

She undid her seat belt and stretched. "There was never a doubt in my mind." The small diner in front of them was doing a brisk business. Red gingham curtains hung at the window and the name BETTY'S was painted in bright yellow letters across the plate glass.

Garrison got out of the Jeep, his appreciative glance following the silky smoothness of Gus's legs. He really should have followed the temperamental water truck into town, just in case it broke down or gave Sam any trouble. But the hell with it. He had done exactly what he wanted to do. He'd got Gus away from the ever-present students and had her for himself for at least a couple of hours. He walked to the diner and opened the door for Gus. If the water truck wasn't in town by noon, he'd go out and see if there was a problem.

Augusta was surprised that breakfast turned out to be an enjoyable meal, with Garrison wagering an extra shower night that he could eat more pancakes than she. She felt starved and daring. She had lost by two pancakes. They were just leaving when the remaining members of the crew piled into the diner. Garrison reluctantly accepted their invitation to stay, but Augusta excused herself. She wanted to sketch the buildings that lined the main street.

She grabbed a blanket from the Jeep, spread it in the shade of a huge tree, and was soon absorbed with her drawing.

After what must have been hours, she suddenly felt Garrison's presence behind her. She turned and smiled at the man casually stretched out on the red wool blanket. "How long have you been there?"

"About thirty minutes." He took the blade of grass out from between his lips. "I was beginning to think you were ignoring me."

She eyed the large sodas and the two wrapped sandwiches sitting on the corner of the blanket. A flush swept up her cheeks as her stomach rumbled.

Garrison chuckled and sat up. "Lord, for a little thing, you sure do have an appetite." He handed her one of the sandwiches. "I took a chance and ordered you an Italian hoagie."

Augusta eagerly took the hoagie. "Thanks. What time is it anyway?" The way her stomach was acting, it had to be twenty-four hours since breakfast.

"You're welcome, one-thirty, and are you sure one sandwich is going to be enough?"

She sank her teeth into the delicious meal and grinned. She swallowed her first mouthful and said, "I'm not a cheap date, you know."

Garrison leaned against the tree trunk and started in on his lunch. "Oh, and is this a date?"

"You tell me? You're the one who insisted like some caveman that I come along with you." She took a sip of soda and delighted in his outraged expression. "You really should practice up on your technique, Garrison. These are the nineties, you know."

"There's nothing wrong with my *technique*," Garrison sputtered.

"Oh?"

He stretched out his long legs, crossed his ankles, and grinned. "It got you here, didn't it?"

Augusta laughed as the group of students rushed across the street and joined them.

"Hey, Doc, can we have next Saturday afternoon off?" asked Randy.

"Please!" Caroline and Stacy pleaded in unison.

Augusta smiled at the group. Garrison looked directly at Ben and asked. "Explanation, please."

"It's the annual Spring Wind-Up dance. This year they're having it in Elmer Spur's barn and we're all invited. It starts around five and lasts the night and well into the morning, according to Elmer."

Garrison eyed his students. They had been working their tails off for the past three weeks with only Sundays off and never a complaint. Everyone needed a break sometime, and Hot Springs didn't offer too much in the way of entertainment. The Spring Wind-Up Dance came only once a year. "That will mean we will all have to spend the night in town. There's no way anyone will be driving that road back out to the Boneyard at that hour."

"Elmer said the men can stay in his bunkhouse. The ladies will have to book rooms at Minnie's."

Garrison shot Gus a quick glance at the term *ladies*. She seemed to be caught up in the excitement of the dance along with the group. "I'll give you guys off Saturday afternoon. If you want to come into town, that's fine by me."

Everyone talked at once. The girls quickly started

discussing what they were going to wear, thanked Garrison, and disappeared down the street toward the drugstore. The boys shouted their thanks, boasted about the amount of beer they could put away, and headed off after the girls.

Augusta watched them go and finished her sandwich. "That was nice of you to give them the afternoon off."

Garrison moved a little closer to her. "I had my reasons."

"You did?"

He moved her sketch pad, pencils, and empty soda can out of the way and slid closer. "I won't be at the Boneyard Saturday afternoon to make sure they're doing the job right anyway."

The rough material of his jeans brushed against her bare leg. "You won't?"

"No, I'll be heading into Hot Springs myself." His finger lightly traced the outline of the delicate blue vein throbbing wildly in her wrist. "I have this urge to hold a certain lady in my arms and dance the night away."

Augusta swallowed hard and licked her dry lips. Heat was flaring up her arm. "You do?"

He picked up her hand and placed a tender kiss at the base of her thumb. "I haven't asked this certain lady if she would join me yet."

"Why not?"

His teeth nipped at the pounding pulse. "She doesn't approve of my technique."

"She's a fool," Augusta whispered breathlessly.

Garrison smiled as he trailed a path of light kisses up her inner arm to the tender spot on the inside of her elbow. "Do you think she'd say yes if I asked nicely?"

Augusta closed her eyes as his tongue faintly traced an erroeneous zone on the inside of her elbow she never knew she had. Lord, when had she developed such sensitive skin? "Yes."

Garrison lifted his lips from their tender assault. Hunger darkened his eyes as he gazed at her sweet mouth. He wanted to lay her down on the soft blanket with the sweet smell of grass surrounding them and love her. But this was not the time or the place to tempt his control. He waited until she opened her eyes before asking, "Will you come to the dance with me?"

Augusta yawned and entered the mess tent. She usually welcomed Monday mornings with a smile. But, then again, she usually slept Sunday nights. Garrison was driving her bananas. Yesterday, after getting her affirmative answer to his question about the dance, he couldn't have moved fast enough to put some distance between them. He had left her sitting under the tree on the pretense of handling more business and the promise to make her a room reservation at Minnie's Motel. She had spent the remaining afternoon shopping for something to wear to the dance, picking up personal supplies, and doing her laundry. Dinner had been a noisy affair with everyone from the Boneyard crowded in the last three booths at Betty's. Garrison hadn't even sat in the same booth, and the ride back had been accomplished in relative silence. He made only an occasional remark about the water truck that was fifty feet in front of them the entire way back to camp.

She reached for the pot of coffee sitting on the kerosene stove and nearly burnt her fingers. With a muttered oath she realized she had better wake up before she did some physical damage to her extremities. An illustrator couldn't illustrate without her hands. Last night after everyone had gone to their tents she had sat at her miniature kitchen table and tried to start the actual writing of her book. Under the harsh glare of the lantern she had ended up doing a sketch of Garrison from memory. It was one of her best efforts. She had captured the little-boy look he wore as he pored over the paperwork in the office. It was also one of her stupidest. She could never use the drawing in one of her books. It was too personal.

She sat down on the bench next to Stacy and opened a box of cereal that was guaranteed to talk to you in the morning. She poured milk over the flakes and listened. Her chuckle caused a few heads to turn and stare at her. The cereal was making more sense than she was.

Stacy passed her a banana and asked, "Are you feeling okay?"

"Sure, just having a friendly chat with the cereal." She peeled the banana halfway down and raised it to her lips.

Garrison stepped into the mess tent and groaned in pure agony as Gus's sweet lips closed on the end of the banana. Every pair of eyes in the tent turned and stared at him. He muttered a curse, quickly turned, and stood in front of the metal food locker, debating what he was going to have for breakfast and trying to figure out how to get his overactive hormones back under control. A rueful smile curved his mouth as he wondered if Tarzan ever encountered this problem with Jane.

"Doc, are you all right?" Ben asked.

He glanced over his shoulder at the student and cringed at the way everyone was still staring at him. He realized that he had been standing in front of the food locker muttering to himself the entire time. Lord, he prayed no one heard anything he had said. "Yeah, I'm fine. Just figuring out some stuff in my head, that's all."

Ben looked unconvinced but returned to his breakfast.

Garrison refused to look toward Gus as he helped himself to some fruit and coffee. In a loud voice he started to outline what he was expecting from the students for the week. They were all going to work on the new site he had marked off last week. He casually ended with the announcement that Augusta would be following *him* around for the week instead of *them* because she wanted to get some drawings of him and what he did all day.

Augusta felt her cereal scream all the way down her throat as Garrison's statement reached her. She was going to be with him the entire week from dawn until dusk. She would have to sketch him doing the things a paleontologist does and keep her personal feelings hidden. Lord, someone give her strength.

Augusta slipped on her nightshirt and yanked a comb through her wet hair. She was tired. She had been on the go since breakfast, and the end was now blissfully in sight. She and Garrison had joined the students all day at the newest site, which he had jokingly stated was so hot it was burning the soles of his boots. One thing she'd learned today was that sandstone wasn't the easiest thing to dig through. They had used jackhammers, picks, and shovels and so far nothing. Not one lousy bone. She had been so discouraged when they headed back toward camp that the students made up a rowdy song about a paleontologist named Russ and his lady love, a thirty-five-ton brontosaurus. Garrison and the group tried to explain they never expected to unearth anything today and that it might even take weeks before a find was made. She had not been impressed; she had wanted to see Garrison's hunch prove correct.

The only good thing that happened was that she got two excellent preliminary sketches, one of Garrison working with the students, and the other of him sweating over a jackhammer. The fine display of his trembling back muscles beneath his shirt had kept her enthralled for hours.

She rubbed moisturizer on her face and hand cream into her hands. Dusk had fallen and she had been the last to use the shower. She could hear the students boisterously discussing something in the mess tent but was too tired to join in the fun. The muscles in her arms were still shaking from her brief encounter with the jackhammer. She had pleaded with Garrison to let her try it. The rest of her body felt disjointed and not quite there. She needed sleep. In fact, she could do with all the sleep she had been missing out on since Garrison had entered her life.

She glanced out of the screen door into the shadowy stillness. The night had cooled off, but not enough to close the inner door. If it got too cold later, she'd close it. With a yawn she shuffled down the hallway, turned down her blanket, and cautiously climbed into bed. She never even remembered laying her head down on the peach-colored pillowcase Garrison had bought her.

Half an hour later Garrison lightly knocked on her door and called her name. Everyone had been gathered in the mess tent having a great time and devouring a cake the paleontologists had brought back from town yesterday, when he noticed that Gus still hadn't made her appearance. She should have been done with her shower and returned a while ago. He had stepped out of the mess tent and frowned at the dark camper. Was she sick? He knew he never should have let her try that jackhammer, no matter how prettily she begged.

His frown deepened when she didn't answer, and he called her name again louder. Was she even in there? Concerned, he opened the door and stepped up into the camper. His eyes quickly adjusted to the dimness, and he spotted her lying across the bed, dressed in an ice-blue nightshirt. More important, he observed the womanly body filling it out. Desire hardened his body and his voice as he groaned her name. "Gus?"

She didn't move. Worried, he turned on his flashlight, and being careful not to shine it directly into her face, made his way into the cramped hall. She looked like an angel curled up on her side and sleeping peacefully. He laid the back of his hand against her forehead and was relieved to find it cool. Her breathing was deep and even, without any signs of problems. The shadowy darkness beneath her eyes gave him his answer. She was exhausted.

Her lips were softly parted, as if expecting a lover's kiss. His gaze strayed to her breasts. His jaw clamped down on his moan as the jutting of her nipples caused his body to react. Either she was cold, or very excited. Considering she was asleep, she must be cold. The hem of her night-shirt was hiked, revealing several inches of thighs. The temperature in the camper suddenly became sweltering, and the air was too heavy to breathe. He needed to get out of there before he did something really stupid. Like crawl in next to her and wake her with a stream of kisses. He'd start with her toes and cover every inch of her until he reached the honey softness of her hair.

Careful not to wake her, he gently pulled the blanket, which was bunched up under her, and covered her. He leaned over the mattress and quietly cranked the windows till they were nearly closed. His lips were feather-soft as they brushed a kiss across hers. "Sleep well, my lady," he whispered into the darkness as he turned off his flashlight and quietly slipped out of the camper.

Augusta glanced from the sketch of Garrison resting on her knees to the actual subject swinging a pick into the hardened earth. Something was different about him. She couldn't put her finger on it, but she noticed the difference the second day out with him. He seemed withdrawn, or as if he was contemplating something of worldly importance. Even the students were picking up on it. For the past three days he had insisted on staying with the students, and today looked like the same itinerary. She was bored and edgy. How many sketches could she do of Garrison jackhammering or swinging a pick? She needed new material. "Hey, Doc?"

Garrison felt her sweet voice cut through his reserve. For the past three days he'd had to put up with her staring at him for hours. It was unnerving and becoming downright impossible to hide his body's reaction to her intense gaze. The way she called him Doc, like his students, grated on his remaining nerves. Dammit, she wasn't one of his students. He lowered the pick and glanced over to the boulder where she was sitting. "Yeah?"

"Are we going to be here all day again?"

"Why?" He noticed that the dark circles beneath her eyes had disappeared days before, and she seemed to have more bounce and energy than he and three of the students combined.

"Everyone has been doing the same thing for the past four days. I can't keep sketching the same scene over and over again." With a wide sweep of her arm she encompassed the entire area. "Even the landscape is becoming boring."

Garrison and the students chuckled at her exasperation. They had never thought of it from an artist's point of view. Garrison looked around the area and realized just how boring it could be from where she was sitting. He leaned on the pick and smiled. "How about if I take you on a hike toward the east? There's an area there I want to check out."

Augusta quickly stood up and dusted off her shorts. "Let's go," she said before he could change his mind.

He couldn't help but grin at her enthusiasm. "Ben, would you mind taking charge and seeing that everyone gets back to camp on time?"

"No problem, Doc."

Garrison replaced some of his tools in his backpack and checked out his gear. With a glance toward Gus, who was busily repacking her stuff, he said, "Put on some more of that sunblock junk."

Augusta flushed as she reached for the bottle of cream. How could the man pick up the slightest tinge of pink on her skin from twenty feet away? He must have phenomenal eyesight. After applying a liberal amount of cream to her exposed skin, she hoisted the tote bag and picked up her briefcase. "Ready when you are."

Garrison finished giving the students some last-minute instructions and headed eastward. His stride was slower than normal, and he tried several times to carry her briefcase. His southern peach was as stubborn as ever, insisting on carrying her own gear and matching him step for step.

The camp was a half hour behind them when Garrison noticed that Gus kept glancing over her shoulder. "Is something the matter?"

"No."

"Then why do you keep looking behind us?"

"We're being followed."

Garrison stopped in his tracks and turned around. Who in the hell would be following them? He didn't see any movement in the distance. "I don't see anybody."

"It's not a somebody, it's a some*thing.*"

Garrison stared at her as if she had just sprouted wings and flown. "What?"

She pointed skyward at the dark, circling bird. "Him."

"It's only a vulture."

"I know what it is. I just don't like being followed by one, that's all. It makes me want to keep checking my pulse."

On impulse, he leaned over and tenderly kissed her cheek. "I'll let you know if there's any chance of attack." Startled by his own actions, he quickly turned and started walking again. He hadn't meant to do that.

Augusta's fingers lightly touched the spot he had just kissed as she followed him. That was the first time he had touched her since under the shade tree in town. Maybe the old Garrison was finally coming back.

Half an hour later she couldn't contain it a moment longer. She had to tell him. "Doc?"

He slowed his pace but continued to study the surrounding landscape. "Hmmm . . ."

Augusta wondered how a *lady* went about telling someone she needed a little privacy. If she was in his class, she could politely raise her hand and ask to be excused. With an apologetic smile she said, "I don't think I should have had that second cup of coffee this morning."

Garrison's confusion cleared up the second he

glanced at her. Why in the hell hadn't he thought of that? He looked around the barren hills and gullies. Not a bush in sight. His lady was really going to appreciate this one. He grabbed her hand and pulled her up the hill on his left. He stood looking down the other side and was glad to see it wasn't a steep descent, or that anything seemed to be living there. To be on the safe side, he withdrew his pick and after a few vicious strokes a small avalanche of stones and debris tumbled down the incline. "There, that should be safe. Anything that was there is long gone by now."

Augusta shook her head. All she needed was a moment of privacy, not for him to rearrange the landscape. "I'm sure I'll manage."

Garrison turned away and started back the way they had just climbed up. "Give a yell if you need me."

Augusta ignored his chuckle as she started to cautiously make her way down the incline. She was a third of the way down when the loose rubble under her boots gave way and she felt herself slip. The impact of her rear connecting with the hard earth caused another landslide. This time she was honored to be in the middle of it.

Garrison heard the commotion and was halfway up the other side of the hill when her scream filled the air. Pure terror gripped at his heart as he crested the hill and saw her lying in a heap at the bottom of the incline.

Six

Garrison started to hurry down the hill, urgently calling her name, only to have his feet slip out from under him. In a cloud of dust and pebbles he slid down the slope to land practically on top of Augusta.

She pushed back a wisp of hair that had escaped her ponytail, blinked at the settling cloud of dust, and smiled at Garrison's head resting on her thigh. Bracing herself on her elbows, she asked, "Gee, Garrison, what took you so long?"

He quickly pushed himself up and asked, "Are you hurt?"

She rubbed her sore posterior. "Only my dignity. What about you?"

"Is my hair completely white?"

She glanced at his dark hair and smiled at the gray dust coating it. "No."

"Then I'm fine." He knelt in front of her and frowned at her legs. They were covered with tiny scratches and gray grit. He gingerly reached out and started to brush some of the dirt off them so he could better assess the damage. Gus was safe and basically unhurt. That was the main thing.

"Can I keep it?" She winced as she brushed off the palms of her hands. They were covered with scrapes and at least one small cut. "I found it."

Garrison looked up and asked, "What are you talking about?"

"You didn't notice! Gee, you must have hit your head or something." Worriedly she asked, "Are you sure you're all right?"

"I told you I was fine. I'm the one wearing thick jeans and a long-sleeved shirt. I'm not the one parading around half naked." He reached for his backpack, and withdrew a small first-aid kit. He opened up his canteen and poured clean water on her scratches.

"You didn't answer my question. Can I keep it?"

He gently dabbed at the red marks. "I don't know what you are talking about."

She pointed to a spot just over his shoulder. "That's what I'm talking about. Can I keep it?"

Garrison glanced over his shoulder and lost his grip on the canteen. Water splashed her shorts as his mouth fell open at the sight of a dinosaur bone embedded in the side of the hill. The part showing was at least three feet long, and it appeared to be in perfect condition.

Augusta grabbed the canteen before more water was wasted and flinched as the cut on her palm connected with the canvas material covering the canteen.

He noticed her wince and gently took her hand.

He muttered an oath at the sight of blood smearing her palm. "Why didn't you tell me?" He took the canteen out of her other hand and cleaned the palm. It wasn't as bad as he had first feared. He opened his first-aid kit and uncapped a small bottle of peroxide. "This might sting a bit, but we have to kill the germs before it becomes infected." He held her gaze as he poured on the liquid. She never jerked her hand or cried out, but her golden eyes pooled with pain and tears. It tore at his heart. He quickly applied a Band-Aid to the cut. When he was done inspecting and cleaning the numerous tiny little scrapes on her hand, he bent his head and placed a light kiss on top of the bandaged cut. "There, all better."

The tears from the momentary pain had long since dried as she smiled back at him. "You do that very well. Had a lot of practice?"

He picked up her other hand and studied it. It was in better shape than the first one. He started to clean it up. "No. You're my first writer who wanted to see what a landslide was like—from the inside."

Augusta chuckled. "Maybe my next book will be about a landslide who wanted to become an avalanche." She glanced at the fossil and frowned. Garrison should have been all over that bone like a mad dog instead of doctoring her scrapes. "I can finish cleaning up. Why don't you go see what I found?"

He ignored the bone. "I want to see you walk first, just to make sure." He got up, dusted off his clothes, and helped her to her feet.

She smiled good-naturedly and took a couple of

steps for him. "There, satisfied?" She brushed off the front of her shorts and top. She wouldn't dare touch the back. Her bruised bottom would be fine walking; it was the sitting down that would cause her some problems.

Garrison watched her walk. No noticeable limps. Everything seemed to be working, except she was very cautious about something. He took a couple of steps closer to her and swiped at the patch of dirt covering her rear.

If there was a roof, Augusta would have been through it. She protectively covered her bottom and demanded, "What are you doing?"

"You're hurt!"

"I'm not hurt," snapped Augusta, "just bruised."

He stared at her shorts and wondered what to do. He couldn't very well demand to see, could he? "Someone should have a look at it."

Augusta glared at him. "Don't say it or I'll pop you one right in the kisser."

"I was referring to Sue Elison, not me."

"I don't need Sue or anybody else to look at it. I'm perfectly capable of knowing where I'm bruised and where I'm not." She started back up the incline. "Go see what kind of bone I found."

Garrison watched as she gingerly climbed up the hill. Nothing seemed broken from the way she was moving. "Where are you going?"

Augusta looked down from the top of the hill and glared. If she'd needed a moment's privacy before the slide and didn't get it, wouldn't it stand to reason she'd need one even more desperately after? "To see a man about a horse." She turned around and disappeared over the crest.

He stared at emptiness for a full minute before the reason finally dawned on him. Gus was not having an easy time of things.

Three minutes later Augusta slowly made her way back to the bottom of the hill using a different route. The one smoothed over by the landslide was slippery and slick. Her poor, bruised body couldn't take another ride like that one. She walked over to Garrison as he carefully tried to remove some dirt from around the bone. "Well, what's the expert opinion?"

"It looks like a femur."

She nodded her head as if in agreement. She wouldn't know a femur from a toe bone. Wasn't a femur a leg bone? "To what?"

"I may be good, but I'm not that good." He painstakingly started to chip at the dirt. "Why don't you give me a hand and then maybe I can see what *you* found."

Augusta reached for her tote bag and pulled out the only tool she had—a small pick. She cautiously sat on a rock and placed all her weight on her left side. At least she could sit down. Following Garrison's instructions, she worked side by side to uncover the discovery of her lifetime.

By noon she decided that being a paleontologist wasn't all that it was cracked up to be. They had barely dented the surrounding sandstone. At this rate it would take her the remaining four weeks of her stay to see what she had found. "Can we break for lunch soon?"

Startled, Garrison glanced up. He had completely forgotten about lunch. The femur was magnificent, a real beauty. He guessed the overall length would be about four feet. But more important was the fact that if there was a femur, the rest of the dinosaur couldn't be too far away. He smiled ruefully. "I'm sorry. I get carried away sometimes."

By the time they returned to camp, the students were halfway through dinner. "Gee, Doc, I was beginning to think you two got lost out there." The other students chuckled at Randy's statement.

Garrison draped his dust-covered arm around Gus's equally dirty shoulders. "Guys"—he glanced at the three female students, and added—"and gals, I would like to present the newest honorary member of our crew."

The students looked bewildered. As far as they were concerned, Augusta had become a member of the crew the day she walked into camp. Granted, she wasn't a student of paleontology, but she always pulled her weight and helped.

Augusta couldn't tell if she flushed because Garrison's arm was around her, or if it was pride. He was finally going to accept her as one of the group instead of some *lady* to be protected. And to think, all it took was one landslide, a prehistoric femur, eight hours of backbreaking chipping, and the sharing of the fruit drink she had tucked away in her tote bag.

"Guess who found what is possibly the greatest fossil of the summer?" Garrison's voice held respect.

Eight pairs of eyes stared in wonder at Augusta. "What?" Ben asked.

"How?" Caroline demanded.

"Where?" Glen and Steve shouted.

Garrison pulled her closer. "It's your story, Gus, do you want to tell them?" He wasn't quite sure how to go about it without embarrassing her.

Augusta recounted the event to a rapt audience. "Doc's still not sure to which dinosaur the femur belonged. We worked on it all day and still haven't uncovered the entire length. Right, Doc?"

Garrison gave Gus a final squeeze, answered a couple of rapidly fired questions the students were throwing at him, and lifted the lid on the pot simmering on the kerosene stove. Canned chili again. The barn dance tomorrow night was beginning to look like a godsend. He'd heard they were going to roast an entire steer and he'd bet that precious femur not one side dish would be from a can. He handed Gus a plate and a silent apology. She shouldn't have to eat canned chili after the day she had just put in. "I want you to take your shower right after you eat. And," he commanded, "I want Sue to look at your bruises."

Augusta grabbed the plate and helped herself to the delicious-smelling chili. After the events of the day, she could eat the north end of a southbound skunk. She had obviously overrated the importance of becoming an honorary member of their crew. Garrison was still trying to wrap her in cotton. "If I thought my bruises needed a second opinion, I would ask someone." She grabbed a spoon and a hunk of bread and headed for an empty seat in the middle of the students.

Garrison stared at her rigid back and sighed. There went the entire peaceful day down the tubes. He had had one of the most enjoyable days he could remember. They had worked side by side for hours, discussing anything that came into their heads. He had learned more about her profession, her family, and the fact that she hated geniuses. He had kept quiet on his I.Q. scores and found himself talking about his family, especially his sister and his two nephews. It was a subject he rarely discussed with anyone because it always left him with a feeling of sadness. If a relationship with a woman was out of the question for him, how would he ever expect to become a father? Today the sadness hadn't come; instead, Gus countered every one of his nephew stories with troublesome nephews of her own.

He had blown the entire day because he was concerned about her health. Well, dammit, what was he supposed to do? Ignore the fact that she could be seriously hurt? He wanted a second opinion on her injuries, and if it couldn't be his, Sue's would have to do.

With a grunt he dished out his own dinner and took the seat nearest to Gus, four places down.

The next hour was spent discussing the femur and the possibility of more bones. Garrison had pinned the femur to a possible five different dinosaurs found in these parts, and two from a kind never found in Montana before.

Augusta stood up and wished everyone a good night. Sunset was approaching, and she needed a shower desperately. She was the last to use it for the night.

Twenty-five minutes later she turned off the water and reached into the hall for her towel. She nearly dropped it when it was held out to her by a very masculine hand. Garrison's hand.

"Sorry, didn't mean to startle you."

She glared at those strong fingers and yanked at the fluffy towel. "You could have knocked."

He continued to stare into the kitchen, giving her all the privacy the small camper would allow. "I did. No one answered."

The slamming of the bathroom door was her response. A moment later she cracked open the door. "Could you at least hand me the nightshirt on the bed?" The door slammed shut again.

Garrison walked to the bed and picked up the shirt. Cool satin ran through his fingers. He lightly tapped on the bathroom door and placed it in her outstretched fingers. He faced the closed door once more. "You could have at least said thank you."

Her voice was muffled coming through the door. "For what? Forcing me to dress in this telephone booth."

He brought in the canvas deck chair from outside and set it in the kitchen. He lit her lantern, opened the well-stocked first-aid kit he had brought with him, and sat on the small cushioned bench against the wall.

Augusta stepped out of the bathroom in her nightshirt and with the towel wrapped around her damp hair. Wishing she had a robe, she marched the two steps into the kitchen and collided with the deck chair. "Ouch, dammit, Garrison"—she rubbed her knee—"didn't I accumulate enough bruises for one day?"

His hungry gaze never left her legs. These were

the same legs that had tantalized him all day. The numerous scrapes he knew still had to be there were barely noticeable. His "sorry" came out sounding like a croak.

She glanced at the open first-aid kit and groaned. The man didn't give up. "Where's Sue hiding?"

"I didn't ask her to come."

Augusta picked up a tube of antibacteria cream, sat in the deck chair, and started to apply the cream to the scratches on her legs. "Why not?" *If Garrison thought he was checking out the rainbow of colors on her behind, he could think again.*

"I watched you during dinner and you didn't seem to be in any pain, just uncomfortable."

She kept her head bent over her leg and shot him a quick glance. "So you are finally going to take my word for it."

Garrison stared at the spot on the wall directly above her head. His fingers were itching to apply the medicine to each and every scrape, and not because he had the urge to fight infection. "I tend to take my responsibilities a little too seriously."

"But I am not your responsibility. I'm your guest."

"The moment you joined my dig you became my responsibility."

Exasperated, she snapped, "Are you doing all this"—her hands indicated the first-aid kit—"just because I'm a *lady*?"

"No. I'd do the same thing for anyone who got hurt."

She shot him a disbelieving look.

"The first week we were out here, Steve slashed his arm. It wasn't deep enough for stitches, so I bandaged him up. I drove him nuts for the next week. Every night I insisted that I check it out and rebandage it."

"Seriously?"

"Afraid so."

She straightened up in the chair and studied Garrison. He had washed up and changed since dinner. He also seemed bound and determined to make sure she was all right. "Why?"

A frown pulled at his brow and a touch of sadness darkened his eyes. "Because I know how merciless this land can be."

Something in his voice alerted her to the importance of the subject. "How merciless can it be, Garrison?"

Her gaze held understanding and the willingness to listen. For the first time in his professional career he told the story of nineteen-year-old Peggy Hunter and her death.

Augusta sat and listened in dazed disbelief. Seventeen years ago a respected university had allowed a young girl, two days into her first dig, to wander off alone to explore. Not only was she ill equipped to handle the rough terrain of the site in Utah, she had basically no survival skills or knowledge. A Girl Scout would have had more knowledge than Peggy.

The information Garrison had gathered afterward stated that Peggy jammed her foot into a hole and managed to break her ankle in three spots. Sometime later a rattler had found an easy mark in the crippled leg and Peggy had died alone in the dark. It had taken the search party two days to find her. Garrison had been with the group as they followed the vultures. The university and the professor were cleared of any wrongdoing, and the case was closed. Garrison had changed schools the next semester.

"Lord, that's terrible." A shiver slid down Augusta's back just thinking about what the poor girl must have gone through. Her hand gently covered his clenched fist that was resting on his thigh. The story of Peggy Hunter had explained so much about Garrison's constant sheltering. He couldn't have been more than nineteen when the accident had happened.

Garrison read the horror clouding Gus's golden eyes and berated himself for putting it there. "I didn't tell you about Peggy Hunter to scare you. I wanted you to be more aware about the dangers."

She squeezed his hand. "I think that was a very difficult story for you to tell, wasn't it?"

He stared down at their hands. One so fair and gentle, one rough and callused. How could he tell her that he still suffered nightmares about it? Sometimes he would find himself running through a misty haze searching for the young student he only barely knew, and other times he would find himself locked in Peggy Hunter's body, feeling all her pain and fears. But the worst nightmare of all was dreaming about one of his own students becoming lost. He returned her squeeze and said, "You're the first person I told about it," and left it at that.

"Thank you."

Garrison cleared his throat. He hadn't meant to get on such a morbid subject. He picked up her hand and turned it over. "Can I examine the cut?"

Augusta would have showed him the brilliant rainbow on her behind if he had asked. "I took the bandage off before the shower to clean it better."

He studied the three-inch-long cut. It was starting to scab, and there wasn't any puffiness or other sign of infection. He took the tube of cream from her other hand and tenderly smeared some on. "Leave it uncovered tonight, but tomorrow put a bandage on it before coming out to the site with us."

"Yes, Doc." She smiled at his commanding tone. Garrison could really be a dictator.

"Don't call me that."

"What?" she asked in confusion, "Doc?"

"My students call me Doc, and you're not one of my students." His fingers came up and brushed her cheek. Her skin glowed from her recent shower, and the alluring fragrance of her soap and shampoo was playing havoc with him. The temptation to pick her up and carry her the three feet to the mattress was nearly overwhelming. He would make love to her all night long and into the morning. They would miss the Spring Wind-Up Dance. Hell, the way he was feeling, they would miss next week entirely.

Augusta felt the slight trembling in his fingers. The spark of desire ignited into a flame. Her unconfined breasts grew heavier and her nipples perked against the cool friction of satin. No man had ever made her feel this way with the merest touch of his fingers. She lightly ran the tip of her tongue over her dry lips. Her voice barely a whisper, she said, "No, Garrison, I'm not one of your students."

He had to get out of there before his hormones overtook what was left of his mind. He had no idea why he had spilled the story of Peggy Hunter to Gus or why he had asked her not to call him Doc anymore. Being called Doc put a safe distance between them, one he would never cross. He had just eliminated that distance. If it was just sex burning between them, he could handle it. But it wasn't just sex, it was something more, something he hadn't been able to label or pin down. Something that excited him like nothing before, and frightened him speechless. Something that he would kill to know what it was, and something he ran from. Tonight was not the night to confront the *something* between them.

He stood up and, ignoring the invitation in her eyes, repacked the first-aid kit. "Will you be all right to hike back out to the site tomorrow morning?"

Augusta stood up and folded the deck chair out of the way. Had she misread the desire burning in his eyes a moment ago? "Sure, it's nothing that a good night's sleep won't fix." She seriously doubted that she'd be receiving a good night's sleep.

Garrison glanced at her and doubted that a night's rest would solve his problem. He picked up the chair and first-aid kit and opened the screen door. Cool night air blew against his heated body. "Great, then I'll see you in the morning."

A frown pulled at the corners of Augusta's mouth as Garrison headed off into the night. Why was he ignoring the pull that was happening between them? Didn't he feel it?

• • •

Augusta nervously smoothed her hands down her denim skirt as the knock sounded on the door of the motel. Garrison was right on time. He had dropped her off at Minnie's two hours earlier with the agreement he'd be back at six o'clock. She had spent those hours wisely. She had quickly showered the gray grit from her hair and body and then filled the tub with steaming water and a generous amount of honeysuckle bubble bath she had picked up in town the past weekend. It had taken every ounce of willpower to haul herself out of the tub when the water had cooled.

She glanced at herself in the mirror as she walked across the room to answer the door. She hoped the outfit she had picked out was appropriate for her first Montana barn dance. The denim skirt snapped down the front and flared. It ended below her knees and she had matched it up with a yellow gingham sleeveless blouse. Her hair was pulled back and tied with a yellow bandanna. She had applied only a minimum of makeup, and her jewelry consisted of a fine gold chain and the same gold studs she had been wearing all week. Coral toenail polish complimented the pair of snappy white sandals gracing her feet.

Augusta opened the door and smiled at the picture Garrison made leaning against the doorjamb. "Hello." He was dressed similarly with brown boots, snug blue jeans, and a long-sleeved light blue shirt. His returning smile could have melted a glacier.

Garrison shifted away from the doorjamb and

muttered a greeting of his own. "You know how to ruin a date, don't you?"

She was confused by the harshness of his words and the pleasure gleaming in his eyes. "Excuse me."

"Here I was, planning on holding you in my arms all night."

"So?" That sounded like heaven to her.

"Now I'm going to have to spend the night beating off all the other men so that I might get near you."

A flush of pleasure swept up her cheeks as she stepped back into the room to retrieve her sweater and key. With a saucy grin she brushed by him on the way out of the room. "Gee, Garrison, you scrub up well yourself."

Garrison was still chuckling as he held the Jeep's door open for her. She sat down and smiled up at him. He shut the door and tenderly caressed her cheek. "What I meant to say is you look beautiful tonight."

Her cheek instinctively turned into his palm. "Thank you, Garrison. And may I add, you look quite handsome yourself."

He bent and placed a light kiss on her mouth. "Keep up that kind of talk and we might not make it to the dance." He released her cheek and headed around the front of the Jeep toward the driver's side.

Augusta glanced at the way the snug jeans were molded to his rear and muttered, "One can live in hope."

Garrison opened the driver's door. "Did you say,

something?" She had either said something about living in hope or living with a dope.

Fiery red stained her cheeks as she looked away. "No, I was just talking to myself."

He started the Jeep and grinned at the embarrassment coloring her cheeks. His lady had said *living in hope.* Maybe he should take her back into her room and ravish her until morning. But he knew that if he and Gus didn't show up at the dance, the crew would send a search party for them. He shot a quick glance at Augusta's enticing calves peeking out from under her skirt. Frustration laced through his body. Tonight was going to prove to be very long and very interesting.

Seven

Augusta snuggled deeper into Garrison's arms and wondered how a country band that could rouse everyone with the liveliest tunes could play such dreamy slow songs. They added the perfect balance to such a magical night. The only thing so far that was missing was the natural conclusion, Garrison taking her back to the motel and staying the night. But the night was still young. It was barely ten o'clock. She was living on hope.

The night had begun with an elaborate spread of food. There had been everything from a whole steer turning over a fire to what appeared to be an entire chicken farm being barbecued. The dessert table had groaned under the weight of every conceivable pie and cake known to mankind. As she sampled everything Augusta had vowed not to eat again until sometime the following week. She had noticed that Garrison did his fair share of emptying the tables. Canned chili might never taste the same after tonight's meal.

The music surrounded the dancers with its embrace. The shadowy corner of the dance area, where Garrison had steered her, was the ideal spot for a seduction. She had never seduced a man before, but then, she had never wanted a man as much as she wanted Garrison. Time was against her. She would be leaving Montana in four weeks. Tonight, if the magic held, Garrison would not be sleeping in the bunkhouse with the rest of the men.

The students had joined up with a group of young people from the surrounding area and had left them alone all evening. The Elisons had mysteriously left the dance two hours before, and Sam Hoffman was enjoying the evening with some rancher's daughter who thought paleontologists were "so . . . cute." As the band started in on another slow song Augusta inched closer to Garrison.

Garrison tightened his hold on the woman in his arms and kept her pressed up against him. She felt too wonderful to let go. His chin nuzzled the top of her head and her breath feathered his chest where the top button of his shirt was undone. If he lowered his head and she raised hers, his lips would be on hers.

He wanted to feel those lips.

His hands clasped her hips and pulled her against his straining arousal. He was tired of the guessing game. Tonight the game would end, and he would discover where this uncontrollable desire would lead them.

Augusta felt his obvious condition pressing against her, and smiled. The seduction was working wonderfully.

Garrison felt her smile against his chest and groaned.

"Garrison?" Her fingers played with the button on his shirt.

"Hmmm . . ."

"If you could have one wish right now, what would it be?"

He closed his eyes as the slow dance came to an end and the lights were turned back up. "Dangerous question, Gus."

She stayed in his arms and glanced up. "I feel dangerous."

Garrison studied her eyes. It wasn't danger she was feeling, but desire. The same desire that was gripping him. "Then my wish would be to be back at Minnie's, discovering what color sheets you have on your bed."

Augusta's gaze never left his as she reached into the pocket of her denim skirt and handed him the keys to the room. "They're white, but you're invited to check it out for yourself."

Augusta didn't remember leaving the dance or riding back into Hot Springs. But they must have because she stood there in the dim glow of the motel's lights watching Garrison unlocking the door to her room. He pushed the door open but blocked her way before she could enter. "Second thoughts?"

She glanced up, looked him in the eye, and said, "Not a one." She stepped around him and entered the dark room. With a few steps she turned on the lamp sitting on the dresser and removed her sweater. She heard Garrison close and lock the door.

His fingers lightly caressed the back of her hand as she laid the sweater across the back of a chair. When she trembled, he stepped closer and asked, "Cold?"

She felt the warmth of his body against her back and shivered again as his fingers teased the sun-bleached hairs covering her arm. She gently shook her head.

He kissed the sensitive area behind her ear and whispered, "Do you know what's been driving me crazy all night?"

Augusta felt a gentle tug on the bandanna and then his fingers in her hair. "What?" She hadn't a clue as to what would drive a man like Garrison crazy.

Garrison buried his face in the silky mass of heaven gliding through his fingers. "Your hair." He breathed in the fragrance. "It smells like springtime." His arm encircled her waist and he tugged her closer as his lips descended on her exposed neck. The collar of her blouse prevented him from exploring her shoulder. "It's not just your hair, it's you." His fingers spread out across her abdomen. "Do you smell like springtime all over?"

If he weren't supporting her, she would have melted into the dark green carpet. She leaned her head back against his chest and lifted her mouth toward his. One word was whispered before his lips covered hers: "Honeysuckle."

Augusta tried to turn in his arms, but he held

her still. Her one arm was pinned down, but with her free one she reached up and sunk her fingers into his hair. She answered the demanding dance of his tongue by standing on her toes and pulling him closer. His fingers slid up her stomach and gently cupped a soft breast. A moan of satisfaction tumbled off her lips, only to be swallowed by his groan of desire.

She stretched her toes to their limit as his masterful fingers undid the buttons down the front of her blouse. Her trapped hand clutched at his thigh.

Garrison felt the gentle squeeze of her hand on his thigh and prayed for strength. His lady deserved more than a quick toss. He might not be able to offer her forever, but he could show her this one night of pleasure. Oh, and what sweet pleasure it was.

He broke their kiss and slowly worked her blouse off her shoulders. His lips moved down her spine and his mouth hovered over the delicate skin at her waist as his fingers found the snap at the bottom of her skirt. With each loud click of a snap undone he placed a kiss higher up on her spine. His lips nuzzled the thunderous pulse pounding in her neck as his fingers teased the last remaining snap.

A flush stained her body from the tip of her coral toenails to the top of her head, and a tremor shook her body as with a finger he traced a circle on her abdomen between the snap still holding her skirt and the lace of her panties.

Garrison undid the back clasp of her bra with one hand and continued his exploration with the other. He slowly drew one strap off her shoulder and kissed the creamy skin. "Your back tasted like springtime." The other strap was leisurely lowered and the same treatment was given to that shoulder. "Will you taste like springtime all over?"

The bra slid to the floor. She arched her back and lifted her arms for him. Garrison raised his mouth from the seductive slant of her collarbone and gazed downward. Hard twin peaks crowned her firm breasts. Transfixed, he gently cupped the treasures.

Her fingers grazed his cheek. "I should, I bathed in it."

Groaning, Garrison released the last snap on her skirt, then swung her up in his arms and carried her to the bed. He put her down in the center of the mattress, stepped back, and hurriedly undressed.

Augusta would have liked to take off his clothes slowly, but she didn't want any more delays. It seemed she had waited a lifetime for this moment. So she contented herself with following his every movement and gazing at the body that would be revealed to her at last. Broad shoulders and a tan chest sprinkled lightly with dark curls tapered into a trim waist. He stepped out of his boots and socks and impatiently wrenched his jeans and underwear down in one movement. Augusta caught her breath at the sight of his arousal, all hard and sleek. She tried to reach for him but her hand faltered in midair. One word made it past the dryness in her throat. "Beautiful."

Garrison felt his chest expand with pride. The woman he desired most in the world thought he was beautiful. Hell, he knew he wasn't beautiful, but at that moment, with the appreciative look shining in her eyes, he felt like a king.

He proudly stepped back to the bed and lifted one of her feet. He smiled at her expression as he removed her white sandal. Now only a provocative scrap of white lace and satin covered her.

A fleeting kiss brushed the inside of her knee. She leaned back and closed her eyes as warm hands inched their way up her thighs. The gentle abrasion of his thumb against the sensitive skin drove her higher into the realm of ecstasy. She whispered his name as her fists clutched the floral bedspread.

Garrison glided his palms upward and brushed his thumbs over the lace and silk shielding her heat. Moisture dampened the fabric. "You're ready for me," he said, his voice rough. Then he slid trembling fingers underneath the elastic and drew the panties down her legs.

Augusta opened her eyes, a whimper of need caught in her throat when he flicked his tongue over her and whispered, "You do taste like spring-time." He raised his head and met her gaze as he slipped a finger inside her slick passage.

She could feel the intensity of the storm building and tried to prevent it. She wanted to wait for him. She needed to be with him when the tempest broke. Feelings such as she had never experienced before were washing over her in wave after wave. They were coming faster and more forcefully with each surge. She couldn't halt their assault. When Garrison withdrew his finger and replaced it with more sweeps of his tongue, the tempest splintered into a million pieces.

Augusta gripped his shoulders as the climactic swells shook her body. For several moments, she couldn't seem to breathe.

Control returned along with the feeling of fullness and rightfulness. Garrison was poised above her, and her hands were still clutching him.

"They say a person's eyes are the mirror to their soul." He tenderly brushed back a wisp of her hair clinging to her damp cheek. "I never believed it until now."

A blush swept up her cheeks and she lowered her gaze. He had watched her as he took her to the brink, and beyond. When Garrison moved slightly, she realized where the feeling of fullness and rightfulness came from. He was buried deep inside her.

Garrison's thumb stroked her lower lip. "Are you ready, my lady?"

Augusta felt the smooth thrust of his manhood and turned her face into the bedspread. "I'm sorry. I should have waited."

He caressed her cheek as he withdrew and thrust again. "That one didn't count." He turned her face and nipped at her lower lip. His next thrust was more powerful and deep.

Augusta looked at him in wonder. Could he mean to do it again? Her legs encircled his hips as the swells began to build in intensity once more. "Garrison?"

He tenderly kissed her. "It's all right, Gus, I've got you. And this time we go together."

Her fingers clutched his back as she matched

his rhythm. Her last word before her cry of ecstasy was "Together."

The pale light of dawn was barely lighting the eastern sky when Garrison was awakened by a string of ticklish kisses across his chest. His body had reacted to Gus's playful mood long before his mind. He was hard, throbbing, and willing to take her to their special place once more. He wasn't quite sure what Gus had been feeling during their final moments of completion. But if it was anything like the streaks of lightning that scorched his soul, then he could fully understand her dazed expression afterward.

He willed his breath to remain even and his eyes closed as Gus's mouth swept lower. He was curious as to how far his lady would take her playfulness.

Augusta knew the instant Garrison had awakened. Her mouth could detect the subtle hardening of his body and the slight change in his breathing. Without a pause she continued her gentle exploration with her fingers and lips. Garrison had dominated last night's loving, leaving her no option but to be pleased. But this morning was hers. Her mouth slid lower.

Garrison felt the warmth of her mouth, jerked her upward across his chest, and captured its heat with his own. His lady wasn't playing anymore, she was dead serious.

She returned his passionate kiss and wiggled her body into a more comfortable position on top of him. Garrison groaned as she broke the kiss and lifted her hips. His breath hissed out between his teeth as she slowly lowered herself back down, surrounding him with her tightness. She arched her back as he filled her and gently rocked her hips.

Firm hands gripped her thighs and held her still as Garrison tried to deal with the pleasure washing over him. The moist velvet surrounding him contracted, nearly sending him over the edge. He released her thighs, caressed the soft swelling of her hips and the indentation of her waist, and slowly tested the weight of her gently swaying breasts. They were perfectly shaped and fit into the palms of his hands as if made just for him. He lightly squeezed their perfection and marveled at the budding nipples poking their way through his fingers, begging for attention. He leaned forward and captured one between his lips.

Augusta's movements became wild as the power between them built. She was unsure who was leading and who was following. It wasn't important any longer. They would reach the summit together. She cried out his name as the crest broke. Garrison's hoarse cry against her breasts, "Augusta," signaled his release.

Augusta regained her breath and snuggled closer to Garrison. Her head was pillowed on his chest and she was listening to the rapid beat of his heart. His warm hand was leisurely rubbing her back. Her eyes drifted closed as Garrison pulled the blanket up over them. All she wanted to do was sleep in his arms. She did not want to think about the fact that she would be returning to

Georgia in four weeks. If Scarlett could get away with thinking about it tomorrow, so could she.

Garrison continued to rub Gus's back long after he knew she was asleep. What in the hell was he supposed to do now? He knew there was something special, something hot that burned between Gus and him. But he hadn't known it was this hot. His refined southern peach had set off an avalanche of emotions inside him. The lady had made her way inside his heart, which would have been better off empty. But there she was, though she would be leaving. It was better that way, he told himself. It could never work between them. Ladies and the Boneyard didn't mix.

With a weary sigh he hugged her and smiled as she nestled closer. For the first time in his life he wondered why he had never listened to his mother, who had wanted him to be a dentist.

Garrison heard the shower start and glanced at the bedside clock. It was after ten. Augusta had to vacate the motel room by noon. He ran a hand over his jaw and grimaced at the prickly stubble. What it must have done to Gus's tender skin. He rolled off the bed and padded naked to the bathroom. The intriguing possibility of inspecting the damage himself was too good to pass up. They had an hour and a half of privacy before stepping out of the room and facing reality.

Augusta returned the motel key with two minutes to spare. Garrison had pitched a fit about not being allowed to pay for the room, but she had held her ground. It was her room and she had invited him in to share the night, not pick up the tab.

She slid into the vinyl booth at Betty's and picked up the plastic-coated menu. She kept it propped in front of her as Garrison continued to mutter about women's rights, the E.R.A., and one southern peach in particular.

A young waitress stopped at their table and asked if they were ready to order.

Augusta lowered the menu and calmly gave her order. "I'll have the deluxe hamburger, french fries, apple sauce, a large iced tea, and a slice of that delicious-looking cherry pie sitting under the glass dome on the counter."

The waitress turned to Garrison, who muttered, "The same for me," and handed her his unopened menu. As the girl walked away he glared at Gus. He really should be mad at her for defying him, but how could he when she was sitting there glowing? He had put that radiant shine in her eyes. She looked like a woman who was well satisfied. "Feeling hungry, are you?"

She drawled, "Yes, sir," and batted her eyelashes at him. "It seems I worked up an appetite this morning."

Garrison threw back his head and laughed. Several patrons, including a couple of students sitting toward the front of the diner, glanced their way. "You're a brat."

"Why, sir, I do declare." Her southern accent was so thick, he expected General Lee to come charging in at any moment. "That's not what you told me this morning in the shower."

He leaned in closer and whispered, "Was that before or after I scrubbed your back?"

"Need I remind you, sir, that you never made it that far?"

Garrison's memory was excellent. His eyes darkened as he remembered exactly what he had lathered and how. Her back wasn't part of the memories. Desire was hardening his body when the waitress placed two large iced teas on their table. He grabbed his glass and downed half the contents. He needed cooling off, but the cold drink wasn't hitting his specific hot spot.

Augusta felt extremely warm even though she was dressed in shorts and a tank top. Deciding that a subject change was in order before she melted the vinyl bench she was sitting on, she asked, "What were you planning on doing the rest of this afternoon?"

Since going back to the motel and making love to her all day didn't seem likely, he said, "I have to pick up my stuff at the bunkhouse. And you?"

"Laundry."

"I have a pile of my stuff in the Jeep. How about you ride out to the bunkhouse with me and then we could do our laundry together?" It sounded very unromantic even to his ears. Who in their right mind would spend a wild night and morning of passion in each other arms, and then do laundry together?

But Augusta surprised him when she gave him a dazzling smile and said, "I'd love to, Garrison."

An hour later Augusta almost took back her

words. Grimacing, she watched as Garrison loaded one washer with jeans, and another with everything else in his duffel bag. An indecent amount of soap was poured on top before he slammed the lids and crammed quarters into the slots.

Garrison stood back and sadly shook his head as Augusta sorted her meager pile into four different machines. Dark colors went into one, lights into another, her towels and sheets were fed into a third, and her lacy, silky delicates were treated to a washer of their own. She even reset the controls on the machine to accommodate their loads, something he never did. Detergent was carefully measured and added before she gently closed the lids and slid quarters into the slots.

They sat down in yellow plastic chairs at the back of the room. "You wasted your money," Garrison said. "All those clothes could have fit into two machines."

She idly glanced at the magazines on the chair next to her. "If I had jammed all those clothes into two machines, they never would come clean. It takes soap *and water* to wash them, and if the machine is packed with clothes, it won't get enough water."

Garrison frowned. He had been doing his laundry himself since his college days and no one had ever complained that his clothes didn't come clean. "What about the environmental factor?"

She flipped through a copy of *Rancher's Wife.* "Such as?"

"Wasting water and polluting the waters with more detergent."

"The machines have water level controls on

them. When I wash a small load, I set it for the lowest level of water. I also decrease the amount of detergent I use." She glanced at a colored photo of a woman delivering a calf, shuddered, and closed the magazine.

He stuck his feet out in front of him and crossed his ankles. He didn't want to be stuck in a dreary launderette for hours, watching the dryers spin. Augusta deserved a better afternoon than this. That was the core of his problem. Augusta deserved a whole lot better than what he could give her. He was mad at her for being who she was, and he was mad at himself for just being himself. His voice was defensive as he snapped, "No one has ever complained about how I did my laundry."

She glanced up from a copy of *Cooking for Your Rancher* and wondered what had gotten into him. He had been acting strange since they entered the launderette. "That's funny. I don't remember anyone complaining now." She went back to reading a recipe for venison chili.

Eight

Augusta sighed, turned off the lantern, and cautiously made her way down the darkened hall to her bed. Garrison wasn't coming. She had left him over an hour earlier with what she considered some very blatant invitations. He obviously wasn't going to take the hint. The discussion he was having with the students on social and family lives of dinosaurs had taken top priority. Great, she had taken second billing to a nurturing tyrannosaurus and a nest full of offspring.

She lay down and kicked the covers to the bottom of the mattress. Her skin was overheated and the satiny smoothness of her nightgown was playing havoc on her nerves. Her body remembered and craved a rougher touch. Garrison's touch.

The trip back to the Boneyard had taken twice as long as usual. The front seats of a Jeep were not built for heated kisses. They had arrived back at camp moments before sundown, frustrated and ready to bite off the heads of nails. So why hadn't Garrison joined her in the camper? He had been acting mighty strangely all afternoon, mumbling and complaining about everything. Whatever was upsetting him had started in the launderette and continued through dinner at Betty's. But the ride home had lightened his mood and heightened his desire. So where was he?

She punched the pillow and willed herself to fall asleep. Lord knows she was going to need it after catching only an occasional catnap the previous night.

Garrison grimaced as the screen door squeaked. He quickly stepped up into the dark camper and whispered, "It's only me, Gus."

No response.

He felt like a thief sneaking around the camp after everybody had retired to their tents and hopefully had fallen asleep. He had even made it to his own tent, stripped, and climbed into his sleeping bag before the insane yearning to join Gus had gripped him like a fever. He had jumped off his cot, pulled on a pair of jeans and sneakers, and headed across the ten feet of dirt that separated him from Gus. "Gus, are you awake?"

He squinted into the darkness and could barely make her out on the bed. She was sound asleep. He kicked off his sneakers, dropped his jeans in the middle of the hall, and crawled in bed next to her. Gus's body instinctively nestled into his warm embrace.

"Garrison?" Her voice was thick with sleep.

"Who else would it be?" He wrapped his arms around her and kissed the top of her head.

The coolness of her cheek was pressed against the warmth of his chest. Her fingers lightly teased a few dark curls. "What took you so long?"

He hugged her close and whispered, "Go back to sleep."

She nestled the curls with her lips. "I'm not tired any longer."

He captured her wayward fingers and groaned. "Listen, Gus, I'm trying to be a gentlemen here." He placed a kiss on her palm and continued to hold her hand.

Augusta giggled. "A gentlemen doesn't sneak into a lady's bed in the middle of the night." She tugged her hand free and stroked his hip. "Especially, naked."

He recaptured her fingers as they were making their way back up his thigh. He groaned as she rubbed one leg over his. The hem of her nightshirt had risen to a dangerous level. "Two minutes ago you were dead to the world."

Her warm lips tugged the nipple peeking through his curls. "Two minutes ago you weren't in my bed."

Garrison rolled over, pinning her beneath him. The movement caused her nightshirt to ride up to her waist. Heated flesh met heated flesh. Before he could lose control, he got off the bed and walked over to where his jeans lay.

"Where are you going?" Augusta reached out and stroked his back.

"Shhh. It's all right, go back to sleep." He tried to tuck the blanket in around her.

She pushed the cover away. "You didn't answer my question."

"I'm going back to my own tent." He lightly kissed the end of her nose. "I'll see you at breakfast, okay?"

"No, it's not okay." She propped herself up on one elbow and glared. "Why are you leaving?"

"I can't have the students thinking we're lovers."

"Why not? I'm an adult, you're an adult, and they are surely mature enough to understand what's going on."

"Think of your reputation."

"My reputation!" The man had a reputation for breaking every rule the university had established. Half the staff considered him an outlaw and a rogue, the other half envisioned him as a folk hero. And to think he was worried about her. "Garrison, I'm twenty-eight years old, not sixteen." She tenderly stroked his hip. "Come back to bed."

He kept his feet firmly planted on the floor. "I have to set a good example. I'm responsible for the students."

She ran a finger down his spine. "Your example was *very* good. Why don't you come back to bed and show it to me again? I'm a slow learner."

Garrison felt desire tightening his body and moaned. Temptation never felt so good. "Think about how it would look if they see me disappear into your camper every night and not leave until the morning."

Her lips followed the same path her finger had explored. "I am thinking of that."

"They would think that it was all right, and the next thing I know they would be tent-swapping and setting up house together." Fiery flames of desire danced across his back and headed straight for his gut. In exasperation he said, "They would be too tired in the morning to get up and dig for fossils!"

Augusta's fingers slipped around his hips and gently held his straining arousal. "Yesterday you didn't seem to have the problem of getting up in the morning."

He quickly turned and wrestled Gus back onto the covers. He captured both her wandering hands and placed them over her head. "That's because they don't have my stamina."

She grinned and ran the heel of her foot up his thigh. "Do tell, sir, do tell."

Augusta settled back against the boulder and tried to get as much of her body out of the sun as possible. Only the soles of her boots were left in its relentless glare. Garrison, who was sitting next to her, wasn't as lucky. He had to pull up his legs to keep them from the heat. She glanced around at the students clustered into groups of twos or threes in whatever shade they could find. Today it had stayed in the high nineties, but it seemed worse with only a few patches of shade for them to rest in. It was a real shame that dinosaur bones never seemed to appear in shade, only in the middle of nowhere.

"Do you have enough water?" Garrison asked.

"Of course. I know all about dehydration and heat stroke, Garrison. I'm not an idiot."

Garrison opened up his backpack and held out two sandwiches. "Want one?"

She smiled and shook her head. The man was addicted to peanut butter and jelly. "No, thanks, I brought my own lunch." She opened up her tote and took out an apple, a pear, and a small box of raisins.

He shook his head at her meager meal. "Are you dieting?"

Outraged at such a suggestion, she snapped, "Do I look like I need to diet?"

Garrison contemplated her luscious body with a leer. There wasn't one ounce of anything on it he wouldn't want there. He wiggled his eyebrows and asked, "Do I look like I need glasses?"

She frowned at the small box of raisins in her hand and absently played with the flap.

He matched her frown with one of his own. Something had been upsetting her all morning. "Okay, Gus, out with it."

"With what?"

He looked around at the barren landscape and the students huddled in the few yards of shade. They had all managed to find shade away from Gus and him. In fact, it was becoming quite obvious that the students were allowing them their privacy. "Whatever is bothering you."

The flap tore off in her fingers. "Besides the point of you sneaking out of the camper this morning?"

Garrison released a heavy sigh. He didn't like it

any better than she did, but he was still in charge of this dig, and he was still the one setting the example. Until he could think up a better way, it was either this way or no way. "I thought we had already discussed that."

"We did." She picked out a raisin, glared at it, and dropped it back into the box. "I'm sorry, Garrison. That was a cheap shot. I understand why you think you have to sneak around, and in a perverse way I even respect it."

He tenderly cupped her cheek and forced her to meet his gaze. "So what really is the problem?"

"You are."

"Me?"

"Why were you so miserable in town yesterday?"

Garrison released her cheek and looked out over the Boneyard. How could he explain his feelings of inadequacy? "I wanted to give you more."

"More!" If Garrison had given her any more, she wouldn't have been able to walk.

He ignored her outcry. "Do you think that after the night we shared I wanted to spend the day doing laundry and shopping? I wanted to take you to a movie, but the nearest theater is three hours away. Hot Springs doesn't have a florist, and a handful of candy bars just didn't cut it. The fanciest restaurant happens to be the only restaurant, Betty's. The choice between pot roast and meat loaf isn't my idea of a romantic dinner." In frustration he threw a stone at an outcrop of rocks in the distance. "I even went as far as sniffing every perfume bottle in the general store while you were buying your fruit." Disgusted, he admitted, "Nothing smelled like springtime."

Tears of happiness filled her eyes. "That's the nicest thing anyone has ever said to me."

Garrison groaned in desperation as her tears pooled. He bent forward and placed a kiss on her startled mouth.

Augusta blinked back the tears and smiled radiantly. She quickly looked around at the students. No one seemed to be paying them any attention, but who cared? Garrison had shown a sign of affection for her in front of anyone interested enough to look. It wasn't much, but it was a beginning.

She picked up her apple and took a bite. Ignoring the drop of juice sliding down her chin, she held the apple out toward Garrison. "Want a bite?"

Garrison glanced at the sweet moisture on her lips to the tempting apple in her hand. A childhood question had finally been answered. He could now sympathize with Adam when Eve enticed him with the forbidden fruit. He captured her wrist and brought the fruit to his lips. Holding her gaze, he said, "You could tempt the devil himself." He sank his teeth into the delicious apple.

Her sweet laughter echoed throughout the Boneyard. "I thought I was."

The nightmare started in its usual way. Garrison knew where it would be heading and tried to wake up before the terror started. But gray mist surrounded him and held him captive.

He saw himself standing on a ledge with a look of pure panic frozen on his face as the mist swirled around his legs like a coiling serpent. The sun was shining overhead, but a thick haze lay three feet above the ground. He looked wildly around him and fought the nightmare harder. This one wasn't about Peggy Hunter and Utah, it was worse. He was standing in his Boneyard. His breathing became labored as he tried to break the bonds of horror. He didn't want to know which student he had lost.

His breathing matched that of his nightmarish image as he stumbled, then continued running through the murky fossil bed. With dread he watched as he cupped his hands around his mouth and screamed the name he didn't want to hear. "Gus!"

His nightmare took on a new, hellish proportion. *He had lost Augusta!* He lay immobile as he watched himself climb hills and slide into mist-clogged gullies wildly calling her name. *"Gus! Gus! Gus!"* He scampered up onto an overhang and looked out across Dead Man's Gorge. With a feeling of dread he knew what he was going to find.

Sweat broke out and covered his entire body as he thrashed around in bed, trying to wake up. He had to wake up. He had to find Gus!

The hideous cries of vultures caused him to look up for an instant before staring down into the gorge. The mist was clearing and a faint outline of a crumpled body lay on the rocky bottom. His scream of terror was ripped from his soul. "Gus!"

"Garrison, wake up!" She shook him again. "Wake up, Garrison."

He mumbled something incoherent and continued to shake.

"Please, Garrison, wake up!" He was beginning to scare her. Her heart was pounding and her damp palms were slipping against his soaked skin. She shook him again. "Garrison?"

He slowly opened his eyes and called her name. "Gus?"

"Shhh . . . I'm here." She didn't know what the dream had been about and wasn't about to ask. The way he had called her name was enough to curdle her blood.

His arms encircled her with a punishing grip. He was awake and Gus was safe.

She returned his embrace with every ounce of strength she owned. After a few moments his breathing slowed and the shivers stopped. "Garrison?"

"Shhh." He kissed the top of her head and kept her pinned against his chest. "Let me hold you for a while longer."

She frowned as her mind answered him, *forever if you want to.* Where had that thought come from? In a few weeks she would be leaving to go back home, two thousand miles away. Forever wasn't supposed to enter into the picture. The beat of his heart picked up speed and his breathing quickened. She raised her head and gently called his name. "Garrison?" She didn't want him to fall asleep and back into the pit of hell.

He cupped her bottom and brought her in contact with his desire. He needed to make love to her. He needed to prove it was only a nightmare and erase it from his mind. Gus was safe and in his arms—and he vowed to keep it that way.

Augusta glared at the ceiling of the camper and cursed. The sound of rain beating down on the metal roof was driving her crazy. If she didn't get out of this sardine can, she would be out of her mind within the hour. The rain had started early the night before and hadn't let up a bit all morning. The only good thing to come out of the downpour was that Garrison had finally allowed her out of his sight for more than five minutes. Ever since his nightmare last week, he had shadowed her every move. At first it was kind of cute, the way he was so protective of her. She had even understood his need, but lately it had been getting on her nerves.

He had left that morning at dawn and joined her for breakfast in the mess tent with the rest of the crew. All field explorations were canceled because of the treacherous condition of the Boneyard. The sandstone couldn't absorb the heavy rains, so the water poured over the rocks and into the dry creek beds, only they weren't dry any longer. She had returned to the camper after breakfast, declaring she had work to do on the book, which was true. Only problem was she hadn't accomplished a whole lot. She missed Garrison.

She gathered up the pages of written notes in front of her and threw them on top of the sketches littering every available inch of kitchen surface. It was no use. She couldn't concentrate on which pictures went with what notes. Maybe what she needed was some sketches of what a paleontologist does during bad weather.

She stood up and stretched the kinks out of her back. Her watch showed it was lunchtime. She grabbed her raincoat out of the bathroom, where she had hung it to drip after the morning's run to breakfast. Her sneakers were still drenched as she pulled them on and made a dash for the mess tent.

Augusta entered the tent and shook the water off herself. When was the rain going to let up? The temperature was in the seventies, warm enough to make everything damp stick to you and to raise the humidity. She returned the students' greetings as she hung her vinyl coat on a peg sticking out from one of the support poles.

Wet green vinyl arms encircled her from the rear. "Yuk! Garrison."

He released her and took off his coat. "I was just about to come and get you." He shook the rain from his hair and grinned at Gus's look of outrage as the drops pelted her.

She pulled her damp blouse away from her stomach. "Try putting up your hood next time. You'd stay drier."

He bent and swiftly kissed the tip of her nose. "But I love getting wet."

A blush swept up her cheeks as she remembered his enthusiasm for sharing her shower, and it had nothing to do with getting wet. She glanced at the students, who were busily ignoring them, and asked, "Aren't you hungry?"

His eyes darkened as he stared at her mouth. "Oh, yes, ma'am. Starved, as a matter of fact."

Augusta stepped away from him and headed for the food locker before she could drag him back to the camper for lunch. She opened the locker and frowned. Two days before their scheduled trip into Hot Springs, and the cupboard was getting mighty bare. She picked up a box of dehydrated eggplant Parmesan and shuddered as she read the ingredients.

Garrison reached for a colorful box and demanded, "Who bought a box of prunes?"

Augusta replaced the box in his hand and sweetly suggested, "Maybe the kids thought you were old and needed them."

He ignored the chuckles coming from the students and picked up a can of stewed tomatoes. What in the world was he supposed to do with them?

Augusta bent over and studied the bottom shelf. "Garrison, do you realize there are seven cans of sardines, twelve cans of pepper pot soup, and a jar of pickled herring in here?"

"All right, who bought the herring?"

She glanced up at him and shook her head. The man favored certain foods and that was that. She wished she hadn't finished her last piece of fruit at breakfast this morning. "How about I heat the soup and you fix some sandwiches?"

"Peanut butter and jelly?"

Exasperated, she headed for the kerosene stove. "Is there any other kind?"

"Of course there is." She glanced over her shoulder at him. He grinned and said, "I just don't eat them."

An hour later she settled into a canvas deck chair in the office with Garrison. The students were in the mess tent busy poring over books, sketches, and assorted scattered pages, trying to categorize some of their recent finds. The job of identifying each and every fossil was tedious, boring, and time-consuming. It was saved for rainy days and the cold winter months ahead. The paleontologists from Princeton had returned to their tents to do some research and categorizing of their own.

Garrison pulled out his sketches and measurements of the femur she had found and scattered them across his makeshift desk. "I'm going to try to pinpoint which dinosaur the femur belonged to." He figured if she was going to sit with him all afternoon and learn what he did during bad weather, he might as well do something that would interest her. He gathered up a couple of books that were spread around the tent and sat down.

Augusta smiled politely and tried to listen to him explain exactly what he was doing. Technical words and data washed over her as she listened to his deep voice. Who cared about Cretaceous or Jurassic periods? Who cared about femurs? Who cared about dinosaurs when Garrison was less than five feet away. As time passed, Garrison became more involved with his investigation and less inclined to talk. Books were opened and abandoned. Notes, papers, and maps were scattered across the desk. She silently sat back and watched.

She looked on in amusement as he jumped up, and with a gleam in his eye started to rip open some packing crates with a hammer. He tore the lid off the first box and dropped it to the ground. With tender hands he reached in and started to unwrap the first fossil, only to place it on the side, and reach for another.

It was in the third crate that he found what he must have been looking for. He cradled the eighteen-inch bone and carried it back to the desk. He lit the lantern and pushed a stack of books out of his way.

Augusta pushed her chair back and reached for her sketch pad and pencils. This was what she had come to capture on paper. The look of total concentration, of wonder, of awe that appeared on Garrison's face. It was almost as if he were having a religious experience. He quickly skimmed a couple pages of text and notes before moving the bone closer to the light.

Her pencil flew across the page as she captured his expression. His concentration was so great, he had forgotten she was in the tent. A smile teased the corner of her mouth as she sketched the firmness of his chin. She lost track of reality the same way when she drew.

Her pencil faltered when she started to sketch his hands. Her gaze was riveted to the strong, callused hands gently holding the fossil. How could sure, masculine hands be so tender? A shiver of desire slid down her spine as the tips of his fingers lightly ran over the rough edges. Those same fingers had caressed her in the same way, gently exploring her every curve.

She swallowed hard as heat poured from her stomach to gather between her thighs. Her breasts swelled and her nipples pressed against the lace of her bra as she watched his fingers stroke the length of the bone. The pencil fell from her trembling fingers to the ground. She wanted those loving hands on her.

A flush stained her cheeks as she tried to control her breathing. The noise of rain hitting the canvas roof sounded primitive and uncivilized. It heightened her senses and escalated her arousal to a feverish pitch. She wanted Garrison now, and he didn't even realize she was in the same tent.

Her hungry gaze drifted over his wrists and up the arms that had held her close all night. His shoulders seemed broader in the yellowish glow of the lantern, and the strong column of his neck cried out for her touch. Her gaze slid over his stubble-darkened jaw, past his sexy mouth, which could give her so much pleasure, and upward.

Garrison felt her exploration and raised his gaze.

Augusta's breath caught as their eyes locked. He would be able to read her secret in her eyes. She wouldn't be able to hide it from him any longer. It wasn't just arousal she was feeling, it was love. She was in love with Garrison.

Garrison lowered the fossil to the top of the desk when he saw the look on Gus's face. It was the same flushed look she wore right before he entered her. "Gus?"

Embarrassment flooded her face as she jumped up, dropped the sketch pad, and ran from the tent.

Garrison stood up and urgently called her name as she disappeared into the downpour. He rounded the desk, hopped a crate of fossils, and ran out after her.

He found her standing in the deluge behind the office tent. Her arms were folded protectively under her breasts as she stared out across the Boneyard. Her blouse and shorts were drenched and plastered to her body. Rain had soaked her hair and ran in rivers down her back and legs. He came up behind her and wrapped his arms around her waist. "Gus?"

She shivered and leaned back into his embrace. The tears of wonder and sadness streaked down her cheeks and mixed with the rain. She had fallen in love for the very first time, but with the wrong man at the wrong time. Garrison wasn't looking for commitments and promises of forever. He had already made those promises—to a bunch of dead beasts who had roamed the earth millions of years ago.

He brushed her hair off her neck and lightly kissed the moist skin. His arms tightened as she trembled against him. "Let's go back to the camper."

She shook her head and continued to stare blindly out across the dreary landscape. What was she going to do now? Hightail it back to Georgia and try to live without him, or stay as long as possible and show him exactly how she felt.

His hands gently cupped her breasts and stroked the hardened nipples through the saturated blouse. He groaned as she arched into his palms. "Gus, we're standing in the middle of a monsoon."

Those hands that had caressed the fossil were finally on her.

Garrison glanced around behind them. Nothing but a curtain of rain and some faint outlines of tents. His fingers hurriedly undid the buttons of her blouse and released the front clasp of her bra. Slick mounds filled his hands to overflowing.

Augusta turned her head and raised her mouth toward him. He took the offering in a heated kiss. She tasted like rain, tears, and springtime. When she turned around in his arms, he held her still and pressed the bulge in his jeans against her bottom. His deft fingers stroked down her abdomen, unsnapped her shorts, and slid the zipper down. Warm fingers and rain slipped under the white satin and lace of her panties to be buried in soft brown curls.

The deep thrust of his tongue caused her to arch her hips upward. He dipped his fingers into her moistness and groaned when he felt her contract around him. She was so ready, perched on the brink of fulfillment. With a gentle thrust of his finger he sent her over the edge.

Augusta raised her arms and cried his name as her body shook relentlessly.

He released her and turned her into his embrace. His body absorbed her tremors as he lightly kissed her cheek. "I've got you, Gus. I've got you."

She buried her face against his wet shirt. Lord, what had happened? One moment she was depressed about falling in love with him and the next she was coming apart in his arms.

He tenderly cupped her chin and forced her to look at him. "Why did you run?" She closed her eyes against his probing gaze. He lightly kissed the lowered lids and her mouth. "Never run from me, Gus. I'll never hurt you." He brushed a wisp of damp hair away from her cheek. "Don't you know what it does to me to give you pleasure?"

Augusta knew she wasn't going to run back to Georgia. She was going to stay and show him her love. There was a good chance he would end up hurting her, but by running she would only be hurting herself. "I won't run, Garrison." She smiled up at him. The bulge in his jeans was pressed up against her stomach. "We could go back to the camper now."

Garrison chuckled and moved away. The little minx was dangerous. "We could, but we won't." He placed a light kiss on her pink nipples before fastening the front clasp of her bra. The pouring rain made rebuttoning her blouse awkward, and it took both of them to zipper her shorts.

"Why not?" She wiped her soaking wet hair out of her eyes.

"Because I want you to remember that your pleasure is also my pleasure." He chuckled as her gaze slid back down to his straining jeans. "I do have one question though."

"What?"

"What caused you to become so . . . um . . . " He was trying to think up a diplomatic word.

"Hot for you?"

He grinned; he liked the sound of that. "Yeah, hot."

She bit her lower lip. Standing in a downpour was not the time to declare her undying love. She gazed up at him and gave him the partial truth. "Your hands."

"My hands?" He looked at his hands. They didn't look any different from any other day.

"The way they were holding the fossil back at the tent was the most erotic thing I've ever witnessed." She reached for his hands and ran her fingers over his calluses. Such strong hands to be so gentle. "I wanted them on me like that."

Garrison grinned and hugged her close. "Oh, lady, stick around. You wouldn't believe all the dinosaur bones I get to handle."

Nine

Augusta hurried from the launderette and threw the two duffel bags of clean laundry in the back of the Jeep. Garrison was due at any moment, and she wasn't ready yet. She glanced at two of Hot Springs' elderly residents, who were peering at her through the plate glass window of the launderette. They must be thinking she had fried her brain out in the Boneyard the way she had run around the launderette, like a chicken without a head, begging the machines to hurry up. She quickly glanced down the street. No sign of Garrison. She grabbed her tote bag from behind the passenger seat and dropped a white envelope on the ripped upholstery of the driver's seat. In a half jog, half sprint she took off down the street. She just might make it after all.

Garrison walked up to the Jeep and placed the box he was carrying in the back. He frowned at the duffel bags. Augusta must have finished the laundry. That sure was fast. Here he had hurried through his shopping to help her, only to find it done. He glanced around the street and wondered in which direction she had headed. His gaze caught the white envelope on the seat.

A grin broke out across his face as he tore open the envelope and a slip of paper and a key to a motel room landed in his palm. His loud cry of delight startled a few pedestrians strolling through town as he read the note. *Hurry before all the bubbles disappear.* Garrison jumped into the Jeep and twisted the key. Minnie's Motel was six short blocks away, and the secret fantasy he had told her about the night before was about to become reality. He couldn't wait to get to her, a tub, and millions of bubbles.

The smell of food woke an exhausted Augusta from her nap that afternoon. She slowly opened her eyes and stared at Garrison's hand waving a foil-wrapped package under her nose. Her sleepy voice rasped one word. "Hamburgers!"

Garrison chuckled and moved away from the bed to retrieve the other packages. His lady had awakened. "'Afternoon, sleepyhead."

Augusta yanked the sheet up to her neck and sat up. "What time is it?"

"Time you ate your lunch before it gets cold." He laid down on the other side of the bed and handed her an icy can of soda.

She glanced at her hand and shuddered. "I still look like a prune."

"I love each and every wrinkle on that luscious

body." He wiggled his eyebrows and grinned wickedly.

"You're just saying that because I knew where all your wrinkles were." Her gaze ran over the intriguing bulge in his jeans. She reached for the cold drink and took a sip. "Can I get dressed first?"

"Nope, this is my fantasy still, and I like you naked." He handed her a hamburger and a cup full of french fries and some packets of ketchup.

She tucked the sheet more snugly around her and unwrapped the hamburger. "But I like you naked too." She bit into the juicy meal.

"When you get around to telling me your fantasy, I'll make sure I'm naked in it for you."

Augusta chuckled. Her fantasy involved him, two hundred wedding guests, and the minister from an old Methodist church in Savannah. Somehow, she didn't think the minister would appreciate Garrison naked during the ceremony.

He raised an eyebrow at her mirth but continued to eat his lunch. One day she would tell him her fantasy and then they could both have a good laugh. "When does my fantasy end?"

She glanced at the clock on the nightstand and frowned. They had only two hours left before they had to head back to camp. "Four o'clock."

His gaze followed hers. Time was his worst enemy. In two weeks she would be leaving him and he was nowhere near ready to let her go. Garrison picked up their food and placed it on the nightstand. They could eat later. He hauled her into his arms and proceeded to demonstrate how thankful he was for his fantasy.

• • •

Garrison turned around for the last time before heading down the incline and out of sight. Gus was still sitting on a boulder with her head bent over her sketch pad. He hated to have her out of his sight, but she had told him she would rather spend the day sketching the students at the dig site than accompanying him in his search for a new one. They both knew it was a test, the only way Garrison would ever get over his nightmare of her getting lost.

Hours later Augusta removed the floppy straw hat Garrison had insisted on buying her in town and wiped the perspiration from her brow. With a smile she thanked her latest model as he scurried over a rock and vanished from sight. The horned lizard had sat perfectly still on the top of a rock for hours, bathing itself under the hot sun. Augusta studied the drawing of her odd-looking friend and grinned. Not only had she sketched the reptile, she had been so mesmerized by his texture that she had added colors and background. She wasn't sure how she would use a lizard in her book about paleontologists, but the creature was too good to pass up. Weren't lizards a distant relative of the dinosaur? As she stood up and stretched she made a mental note to ask Garrison.

She worked the kinked muscles in her shoulders and glanced around the deserted landscape. A frown pulled at her mouth as she shaded her eyes against the late afternoon glare. Where were the students? Not a soul was in sight. She carefully wrapped her finished drawing and repacked her tote. Studying the rocky terrain, she wondered, *Now, if I were a student, where would I hide?*

An hour later she had given up the search. She had circled the area. Nothing. She had climbed up the tallest hill. Nothing. She had even gone as far as trying to find a trail, a footprint, or something that would tell her in which direction they had headed. Nothing. She would make one hell of a lousy Indian. With a weary sigh she dropped her tote bag onto the ground and placed her hands on her hips in frustration. Boy, was Garrison going to be mad at her for losing the students.

With no other option left, she picked up her gear and headed for camp. It was her night to cook, and she had planned on something special, something that took a little more time than opening a can and dumping its contents into a pot. She glanced behind her again. No sign of the kids.

She wasn't worried about them finding their way to camp, as Ben, who was always Garrison's second in command, was with them. She just hoped they would all make it back to camp before Garrison did, because if he found out they had wandered off on their own, their ears would burn from his lectures on safety and the buddy system. Sometimes Garrison acted like a fanatic on the subject. He ought to learn to trust the students a little bit more and allow them a bigger slice of freedom.

Augusta slipped on her sunglasses. It was a good hour's walk to camp. Her steps were sure and bouncy as she thought about dinner. She hoped everyone liked Italian.

Garrison topped the hill and grinned. He found them. He had been hoping to meet up with the group on their way back to camp, and he had. Fortune was smiling down on him today.

He glanced around the distant group and tried to pick out Gus's floppy hat. The students looked to be in a heated argument about something. If there was an controversy going on, he knew his lady had to be right in the middle of it. His lips hardened into a frown as he hurried across the distance. He couldn't see the hat or Gus's silky hair catching the afternoon sun. Where was she?

Ben looked at the group of worried students and tried not to show his own concern. Survival and search skills had been drilled into him since the first day he attended one of Doc Fisher's classes. If everyone kept their heads and did their job, they would find Augusta before dark. "Glen, you and Pam head north. Randy and Stacy east, and Harry, you and Steve go south. Caroline and I will go west. I want everyone to hike for thirty minutes, then head due—"

"Where in the hell is Gus?" Garrison's voice snapped through the group like a whip.

The students jerked around and faced their second biggest fear, telling Garrison they had lost Augusta. Ben quickly glanced at the other students and swallowed. No one seemed inclined to give their professor the news. It was left up to him. "We lost her."

The color drained from Garrison's face. "Lost her!"

"Yes, sir." Eight pairs of guilt-ridden eyes studied the ground.

"When?" Panic caused his voice to rise. "Where?"

Ben took a deep breath and blurted out, "We don't know, sir."

Garrison tried to think. "When or where was the last time you saw her?"

"About one o'clock at Rainbow's Pass," Randy said.

"I remember seeing her after that at Bear Claw Gorge," came from Caroline.

"She was with us at Death Valley," Harry added.

"We were at Death Valley before Bear Claw Gorge," Ben said.

Garrison groaned. He had left the students exploring an area; instead, they had taken a walking tour of practically the entire Boneyard. Gus could be anywhere. He glanced at the kids. Fear and distress marked their youthful faces. The girls looked ready to cry, and even some of the boys had a suspicious gleam of moisture in their eyes. Hell, if he wasn't so scared, he'd cry too. Ranting and raving at the kids now wouldn't find Gus. He needed their help, not hysterics.

Garrison studied the sky and their most powerful enemy, darkness. They had only an hour or so of daylight left. To engage in a search of the Boneyard after dark would be insane, if not suicidal. "Ben, are you positive this is the most centrally located point?"

"Pretty sure."

Garrison looked into the young man's eyes. Fear

and failure shone there. He remembered the feeling of helplessness he had had when Peggy Hunter was reported missing. The professor and two other, presumably competent adults had panicked, causing mass confusion and delay in the search. Garrison had vowed that if an emergency ever arose in his camp, he would handle it with knowledge, skill, and, hopefully, grace. How was he to know that the emergency would involve his own heart? He mustered a confident smile. "Okay, guys, I want you to check your own backpacks for supplies." He glanced at his watch. "We'll meet back here in one hour."

The students started going through backpacks and checking canteens.

Ben strapped on his knapsack and started heading west with Caroline. He turned around and asked, "Where will you be, Doc?"

Garrison moved his backpack into a more comfortable position. "I have a couple of hunches to check out. Don't worry, I'll be back in an hour."

Ben nodded and turned back around.

"If I'm not, you wait for me." In an hour their light would be gone, and Garrison didn't want the kids to try to make it back to camp without him. He buried his face in his hands and tried to think when was the last time he had checked Gus's flashlight batteries.

He watched the kids go and wiped the sleeve of his shirt across his eyes. He never should have trusted the kids with Gus's safety. She was his responsibility, not theirs. He shifted the weight of his backpack and hurried off in a southeasterly direction. Why hadn't he ever questioned Gus on what survival skills she possessed? *Because you thought you could take care of everyone and everything.* Garrison called himself a couple of colorful names and lengthened his stride.

Gus had once said she knew how to read a compass, but Catherine had claimed she could too. When he'd questioned Catherine, she had delightfully showed him how the "little arrow thing" always pointed north. *"Wasn't that just amazing!"* He had no idea if Gus could actually read a compass.

He knew Augusta was an intelligent and quick-thinking woman. But was it enough to survive out there in no-man's-land? Was it enough to beat his nightmare? His pace quickened as he headed for Dead Man's Gorge, the sight of his nightmare. The grim reaper had won once. He would not be winning again as long as Garrison had a breath left in his body to fight.

An hour and twenty minutes later Garrison joined the disheartened and troubled students. He quickly scanned the group and forced his expression not to betray his fear. Gus was not with them and the last light of the day was slowly fading into darkness. Dead Man's Gorge had proved mercifully empty; not even a vulture circled above. He took the long way back and checked out a couple of other potentially dangerous spots, Rattlesnake Gulch and the Bone Cellar. Nothing. Not a sign of Gus anywhere.

He looked at Ben, who sadly shook his head. "Okay, guys, don't worry. We'll find her." He grimaced as his banged-up knee took his full weight. The slide down a steep hill a half hour before hadn't slowed him down one bit. He hadn't even stopped to check out what kind of damage he had done to it. He didn't care. "We'll head on back to camp and call out the reinforcements."

Caroline bit her lip and wiped the tears streaking her face. "Who?"

"The ranchers. They can be here by first light and cover a lot more territory on horseback than we can on foot."

The group avoided eye contact with each other as they all glanced out over the hills and gullies. Night was upon them, and they knew Augusta would have to stay wherever she was until first light.

The students gathered up their backpacks and headed for camp. Ben stopped and glanced behind him. Garrison had his back toward them and was staring out into the shadows. Ben quietly approached and laid a hand on his shoulder. "Come on, Doc. The sooner we get back to camp, the sooner we can call in those reinforcements."

Garrison nodded his head and heard Ben walk away. He couldn't have answered the boy. Tears had clogged his throat. He didn't want to leave Augusta alone out there. Visions of Peggy Hunter's crumpled body haunted his mind. He pressed the heels of his hands against his eyes and willed the horrible pictures away.

He turned from the barren landscape and quickly followed the students. There was a military base a few hundred miles away; maybe he could persuade them to make a couple of passes over the Boneyard in their helicopters. The helicopters would be equipped for nighttime flying and have huge spotlights. He couldn't leave Gus sitting out in the Boneyard overnight. His lady was lost, scared, and maybe hurt. And it was all his fault.

The hike back to camp normally would have taken seventy-five minutes. They made it in under sixty and in the pitch dark. They crested the hill and saw the camp. Lanterns were burning only in the mess tent. Everything else was in total darkness.

They headed for the mess tent, which would serve as the operation headquarters during the search. The students entered the tent one at a time, only to stop in their tracks and gasp in shock. Garrison smacked into Ben's back. "What the hell?"

He looked around for the source of the kids' shock and felt his heart burst with joy. Augusta stood by the kerosene stove, glaring at them.

Augusta counted heads as the students walked into the tent. All eight kids, with Garrison bringing up the rear, were safe and sound. She had been worried sick when they hadn't returned by nightfall, but Barry and Sue had convinced her that she was overreacting. Garrison and the students all knew how to take care of themselves and would be returning soon. They had probably made some great discovery and didn't want to leave it until the last possible moment.

The constant worry of the past hour hardened her voice and made her miserable. She planted one fist on her hip and waved a wooden spoon at them. "Well, I hope you all like burnt meatballs and soggy noodles."

Ten

Garrison's joy turned into confusion as he eyed the wooden spoon. What was Gus so upset about? Wasn't he the one who had just spent the last two hours frantic with worry? He stepped around the students and moved farther into the tent. "What in the hell are you doing here?"

Augusta dumped the already-cooked spaghetti back into the pot of boiling water to reheat. Thanks to their lollygagging, her special Italian dinner was going to taste like paste. "Where else would I be?"

"Lost in the Boneyard!" thundered Garrison.

Startled, she glanced up. "Lost!" Offended by the mere suggestion, she snapped, "I have you know that I've never been *lost* in my life." She started scooping the paste from the pot and piling it on plates. "Whatever gave you such an absurd idea?"

Garrison clenched his fist before he could start pulling all his hair out by the roots. Gus was driving him insane. "Where have you been for the last two hours?"

"Standing over an ancient battered stove, trying to cook a special dinner for thirteen people." She glared at him and shook the fork she was spearing the noodles with. "Nine of which never bothered to show up on time."

"Dinner! Is that all you can think about?"

She placed two meatballs and sauce on top of a pile of spaghetti and shoved the plate at the nearest student. "No. I'll tell you what I've been thinking about. I've been worried sick that something happened to one of the kids and about how mad you'd be at me for allowing them to wander off by themselves." She filled another plate and thrust it at Randy, who took it with a murmured "thanks." "I've been thinking about how you should have been back hours ago and that something awful must have happened to you." Her voice rose as she thrust another filled plate at Stacy while continuing to glare at Garrison. "I've been thinking about every horrible thing that could have happened to you out there!"

"Me! You thought something had happened to me!"

"What else was I to think? You've never stayed out this late before."

"The reason I'm so late is that we were out there searching for you."

"Me! What in the world would I be doing out there in the dark? For heaven's sake, Garrison, you know how dangerous the Boneyard could be at night."

"That's precisely why I was going out of my mind!"

Augusta stopped dishing out food and glanced around at the quiet students. They looked exhausted and filthy. Half of them were busy pushing the food around on their plates and the other half avoided making eye contact with her. "I'd got so caught up in drawing a lizard south of Rainbow Pass that I didn't notice when the students continued on in their explorations. By the time I realized they had wandered away, I had no idea how much time had elapsed or which direction they had taken. I searched for them in the general area, but I couldn't see them. Instead of wandering aimlessly through the Boneyard trying to find them, I headed back to camp to start dinner. I had total faith in them to find their own way home." Her gaze locked with Garrison's. "Why didn't it occur to you to see if I'd made my way back to camp before you started searching?"

He endured her questioning gaze and answered as truthfully as possible. "It never crossed my mind that you would have returned to camp."

"Why not?" She saw her answer in the depths of his eyes. He didn't think she knew how. "I told you I knew how to read a compass." Her hurt glance swung to Ben, who was studying the tips of his hiking boots. "I remembered telling you I could lead the group back to camp anytime you needed me to." She turned back to Garrison. "You didn't think I could find my way back, did you?"

No, in all honesty he didn't think she could, but he was happy that she had. The thought of her being stranded overnight out in the pits of hell was more than he could stand. He didn't care how she did it, just as long as she was safe. "No, I didn't. But I'm sure glad you did."

Augusta felt her world start to tremble. The man she loved had no confidence in her abilities. For the past weeks she had been trying to show him she could handle any situation his cherished Boneyard could throw at her. She had wanted to prove she could mix in with his work as well as the students. Had she failed so miserably? She glanced at the female students and asked Garrison, "Do you think any of them could get lost out there?"

He glanced at the three young women. "It's not an impossibility, but I would have put money on them finding their way back to camp on their own."

Augusta's voice grew husky with unshed tears. "But not me."

Garrison ran a frustrated hand down his stubbled jaw. He hated to hurt her with the truth, and it tore at his gut to admit it, even to himself. "No, Gus, not you."

"Why?"

His fingers reached out to touch her cheek. "Because you're a lady." He sighed as she jerked back from his touch. He shoved his hands into the pockets of his jeans.

Augusta blinked back the tears as she stared at him. This was the end. He would never accept her into the Boneyard or into his life. A lady had no business being in the Boneyard, and he wanted no business out of it. She angled up her chin in a defensive motion and said, "I won't apologize for who or what I am, Garrison." She placed the fork down and scowled at the food boiling away on the stove. The mere smell of it was making her sick. "If you all would excuse me, I'm really beat after the day I just had." The tears were threatening to overflow as she made her way to the tent's opening. "Enjoy your meal. I'll do the cleaning up in the morning."

All eyes were glued to her back as she disappeared out into the night.

Sue Elison finished dishing out the food. The students all sat and at least pretended to eat. Garrison had yet to turn from facing the opening through which Augusta had just walked. "Garrison, come and get something to eat," Sue finally said. "Augusta went through a lot of trouble to make this meal."

Garrison turned around and scowled. He didn't want to eat. He wanted to go after Gus and tell her everything was going to be okay, but he couldn't lie to her like that. Everything wasn't going to be all right. She didn't belong out in the fossil beds digging up dinosaurs, and he didn't belong on some veranda drinking mint juleps, discussing some cotton crop. Their paths through life led in opposite directions. Maybe it was better to end their relationship now before it went any further.

He glanced at the bubbling pot of meatballs and sauce. Leave it to Gus to prepare something different. Never in all his years of digs had anyone made spaghetti sauce from scratch. Until Gus. His gaze slid over the loaves of bread, the butter, and a jar of grated Parmesan cheese. His Gus had pulled a miracle in the food department, but the real coup de grace was the cake. It was three layers thick, at least fourteen inches across, and frosted on the top was some baker's rendition of a brontosaurus. Now he knew what she had guarded so zealously in all those bags she had picked up in town two days earlier. Augusta had gone through a lot of trouble and expense to prepare this meal for them.

Sue poured Barry, Sam, and herself another cup of coffee and sliced into the cake. Augusta had refused to allow them to cut into it before the students' and Garrison's return. "I think you did her and yourself a grave injustice tonight, Garrison."

Garrison slammed his plate on the table and glared at Sue. He didn't need or want her opinion. He wasn't blind. He had seen the tears and hurt in Gus's eyes as she had walked out of the tent. He straddled the bench and stabbed at a meatball with his fork. It rolled off his plate and onto the floor. Well, great! Even Gus's meatballs were blaming him for upsetting her. He'd known it would never work and that he should stay away from her, but would his body listen to reason? Hell, no! He'd had one little kiss and *bam*, his body had demanded more. Well, he'd gotten more, and then some. Now the problem was that it still wasn't enough. It would never be enough. He wanted what he couldn't have. He wanted forever.

He pushed his plate away and stood up. He couldn't eat a bite. Hell, he couldn't even think straight. Without saying a word, he stormed out of the tent. Eleven pairs of curious eyes watched his exit.

• • •

Augusta stared up into the darkness at the bottom of the cabinets above the bed. It wasn't a genuine ceiling, but it would have to do. Some of her best conversations were held with the bedroom ceiling back at her apartment in Georgia. Ceilings made a great sounding board. They were open-minded, never interrupted, and best of all, they never offered unasked-for advice.

She shouldn't have run from the mess tent. What she should have done was start to hurl meatballs at Garrison until he saw the light. They belonged together. Be it in his Boneyard, out of the Boneyard, or when they were one hundred and five, lying side by side in some other boneyard, they belonged together. Running to hide and cry her eyes out in the camper was not going to make Garrison see the truth. She should have stood firm and whacked him with a couple of home truths, the first being that she loved him. Garrison would have been so overwhelmed by her declaration that he'd proclaim his love, get down on bended knee, and ask for her hand in marriage.

Augusta chuckled for the first time in hours. It was hers and the ceiling's favorite game—the would-have, could-have and should-have game. Garrison would no more get down on bended knee than she would have sat on a boulder in the middle of the Boneyard and waited for someone to rescue her. Rehashing the past wasn't going to make Garrison see that they were compatible and that she could fit into his life. She regretted that for two hours he had really thought she had been lost out there. With his experience with Peggy Hunter, she couldn't imagine the visions he must have conjured up. Somehow she knew his nightmare had something to do with Peggy, the Boneyard, and her. Lord, she hoped he didn't dream she would become lost in the Boneyard and end up like poor Peggy Hunter.

A shiver caused Augusta to pull up the blanket. Garrison's skin had had a grayish cast to it when he had entered the mess tent, but by the time she had stormed out of the tent it had changed to bright red. She knew her own complexion had to have been bordering on a pasty white with all the worrying she had done about him and the students. Maybe if she hadn't been so worked up about them being in trouble, she would have been calmer. It wasn't that they thought she had been lost that was so upsetting. It was the fact that after four weeks of telling and demonstration that she could fit into his life-style, at the first sign of trouble Garrison had immediately presumed she couldn't handle it. He had never even given her the benefit of the doubt.

Augusta wiped the moisture gathering in the corner of her eye. The tears were gone. She had had a good cry when she left the mess tent and it hadn't solved anything. All those tears hadn't made her feel one ounce better. What she needed was action, or at least a plan. She had two weeks left to prove to Garrison that not only could she fit into the Boneyard and his work, *but* she could make it a better place.

In the darkness she reached up and touched

the ceiling. The pale light from the moon barely penetrated the camper. Her apartment had moonlight, streetlights, distant sounds of traffic and people, and the faint glow from the night-light in the hallway. The camper was either lit by her lantern or was pitch dark. She had lain in bed and listened as the students left the mess tent and bid one another good night. The camp had been in total silence and darkness for the past hour.

Her breath caught in her throat as the crunch of footsteps sounded outside the windows. Garrison was coming! She'd know his step anywhere. The steps halted by her door. Moments later they retreated into the night. He never tried the door. Augusta reached up and punched the ceiling.

With a muttered curse she jammed her stinging knuckles into her mouth. She had always been a fighter. She had had to fight for her choice of careers, she fought constantly with her overprotective family, and now it looked like she had to fight for the man she loved. How did one go about combating a man's belief that they were totally wrong for each other?

A slow smile curved her lips as an idea began to take form in her mind. She snuggled down deeper into the mattress and pulled the blanket up higher. She whispered her idea to her confidant, the ceiling, and fluffed the pillow in preparation for a good night's sleep. The ceiling had wholeheartedly agreed with her.

Garrison marched over to the camper and glared down at the woman who looked totally at peace with the world. "What in the hell are you trying to do, drive me out of my mind?"

Augusta shaded in just a touch of blue to the harsh landscape. There, now it was perfect. "The only thing I'm trying to do is finish some of these drawings before I leave. Once I'm back in Georgia, it will be hard for me to compare colors."

He stiffened at her reference to leaving. For the past three days she had stayed in camp during the day instead of traveling with him or the students. He had been slowly going out of his mind missing her. "Don't you need to go back out there for something?"

She flashed her most radiant smile up at him. "Well, thank you for inviting me, but I have plenty of preliminary drawings to keep me busy till I leave."

Garrison jammed his fingers into the rear pockets of his jeans. Her smile was intoxicating. Her mouth was pure temptation. He had tasted its sweetness and now he thirsted for more. She looked so breathtakingly beautiful sitting out in the middle of this godforsaken country.

Augusta selected a deeper shade of gray from her pastels. She clasped the chalklike stick and prayed Garrison didn't notice the slight trembling of her fingers.

"Do you have everything you need?" he asked.

No. I need you. "Yes, the students have been quite helpful." She nodded to an old blanket that Randy and Harry had strung up from the camper to form a shady area for her to work under. She now had the advantage of brilliant daylight without having to sit directly in the sun for hours. For the past three afternoons she had sat under her awning, sipping a cool drink and missing Garrison. Her plan to make herself absent from Garrison's daily life seemed to be working somewhat. With each passing day his temper had grown shorter, and he had developed an unusual habit of walking around camp long after everyone else had retired to their tents for the night. Sooner or later he was bound to blow, and she was determined to be there to catch the pieces.

Garrison frowned at the makeshift awning. Why in the hell hadn't he thought of that? Ever since the night they'd thought they had lost her, the students couldn't do enough for her. They saved her a seat in the middle of them at breakfast and dinner. Every evening a group of them sat around in front of her camper, talking, telling jokes, or relating every detail of their day to her. And every evening he found himself sitting alone in the office with a book propped up in front of him, trying to listen to their every word and catch the sound of Gus's laughter. He knew it must be his imagination, but her laughter seemed more forced and less spontaneous than when she first came to the Boneyard. Looking at her now, one would think she was the most contented person on the face of the earth.

He glanced over at the students, who were packing their lunches, checking their backpacks, and waiting for him. His time was running out. He had to be going soon. "I think I've identified the femur bone you found."

A reddish-brown pastel shook in her fingers as she placed it back in the box. "A tenontosaurus, right? The kids told me. They even showed me a picture of one." She shivered slightly and pretended to concentrate on the drawing sitting in front of her. She hadn't the foggiest notion what to do next with it. The entire drawing could have come from the Sunday comics as far as she knew. "I'm just glad he was dead for millions of years before I stumbled across him."

"Oh, I'd say at least one hundred sixteen million." He chuckled at the thought of anyone accidentally *stumbling* across a twenty-foot two-ton dinosaur in Montana.

Augusta looked up and smiled. Without being told, she knew exactly what he was thinking. No one went around stumbling over dinosaurs.

Garrison felt her smile clear down into his hiking boots. Lord, he had missed her the past three nights and days. The Boneyard just didn't seem the same without her brightening it up like some exotic southern flower. He missed the heated look that darkened her eyes when she was aroused. He missed the sound of her laughter and the way her breath caught when he nuzzled the inside of her thigh with his jaw. He missed the sweet warmth that surrounded him when they made love. Lord, if he missed her this much and she wasn't more than ten feet away from him, what was it going to be like when she went back to Georgia?

Augusta nervously shifted in the deck chair. Garrison hadn't spoken more than three sentences to her since the night in the mess tent, and now he seemed reluctant to leave. Had he missed her as much as she missed him? "I have some extra drawings, if you would like one or two."

Great, she'll be two thousand miles away and I'll be left with nothing but a couple of fourteen-by-seventeen drawings to stare at. "That would be great." He studied the drawing clipped to a portable easel. It was a powerfully intense portrait of Ben. He was surrounded by the vastness and the desolation of the Boneyard. The drawing allowed the viewer an intimate glimpse of the solitude of being a paleontologist. Gus's illustrations all held one sharp element, the truth. Nothing was rose-colored and nothing was dressed up to look better than it was. Gus drew exactly what she saw—a harsh, unmerciful land that gave up its buried treasures only with backbreaking work and sweat.

Augusta examined the drawing on the easel and wondered if Garrison saw what she saw. "If you stop by tonight and pick out the ones you like, I could add some color to them for you."

There wasn't anything suggestive about her invitation, just a plain, friendly offer. So why was his heart doing the tango in his chest? "After dinner okay with you?"

"Sure, anytime."

The sound of the students piling out of the mess tent filled the camp. Garrison glanced over at the crew, and for the first time in days smiled at them. He wasn't pleased with their noisy reminder that his time was up with Gus, but they all looked eager to start the day. He couldn't have asked for a better group of students. Garrison signaled Ben that he'd be there in a minute.

Augusta glanced at the students and waved.

They were off to conquer the world, or at least put another dent in the Boneyard, while she stayed back at camp coloring their world for thousands of boys and girls to see.

Garrison's gaze drifted to the bottom of her shorts. Creamy tan thighs disappeared up into the denim material. He shifted his weight to relieve some of the pressure building in his jeans. "Are you going to be all right here alone?"

She shot him a hard look from the corner of her eye. Was he going to start on that again?

He ran a hand down his jaw. He hadn't shaved in three days; there hadn't been a reason to. "I didn't mean it like that." He noticed her shoulders relax. He couldn't help it, he was still worried about her being alone all day in the middle of nowhere. For the past three days the hardest thing he'd had to do was to walk away from camp and leave her behind. He had done it, but it surely wasn't getting any easier as the days went by. "You know what to do if—"

"Yes, Garrison, if a herd of rattlesnakes slink their way into camp, I'll chop off their heads, make a cute necklace from their rattles, and serve rattlesnake stew for dinner."

A dull flush swept up his face. How had she known that he was going to mention snakes? "You don't have to be so smart about it." He watched as the students started to head out of camp.

"Garrison, I don't mean to make light of your concerns. But as I've been telling you for weeks, I can take care of myself." A sad smile pulled on her lower lip. "One of these days you will believe me."

He ran a frustrated hand through his tousled hair. He wanted to believe her; hell, he'd give up his prized tyrannosaurus rex skull to believe her. Maybe he had been digging in prehistoric dirt for so long, it had clogged his brain with primitive ideas about men protecting women. He lifted his backpack and swung it over his shoulder. His anxious gaze shifted to the students. He had to go. "Hell, Gus, I can't help the way I feel."

Augusta watched as he started to walk away. Their time left together was rapidly slipping by. Taking a deep breath, she called, "Garrison?"

He stopped and turned.

"It's all right to feel overly protective for certain reasons."

Dazed by the change in her thinking, he yelled, "Name one."

Her voice floated over the distance between them, carrying one word. "Love."

Garrison's heart stopped. Had she said what he thought she'd said? He was taking a step back toward her when Randy's voice stopped him. "Hey, Doc, are you coming or not?"

He glanced between Gus and the group of students waiting for him. He had to be mistaken about what she had said. Hadn't he? With a curse against time, responsibilities, and dinosaurs in general, he headed out toward the students.

Augusta watched him disappear over a ridge and smiled. The way he kept glancing back at her had shown how undecided he was about leaving with the students. It was all right that he honored his responsibilities to the kids. It was one of the things she loved about him. And she had a feeling he was going to be completely thrown off balance when he came to pick out his drawings.

She unclipped the paper from the easel and replaced it with another. The portrait of Garrison tenderly caressing the dinosaur bone in the office on the day it had poured stared back at her. With a steady hand she picked up a pastel and started to shade his jaw.

Eleven

Garrison picked up a rock and pitched it at the boulder sitting forty yards away. *Thack*, another bull's-eye. His aim had improved since the morning. The students were half a mile away, excavating the tenontosaurus site and trying to locate a few more bones. He was supposed to be exploring the area and locating the obvious hot spots. The only hot spot he could find was the one burning in his gut. The thought of Gus leaving was ripping him apart inside.

For four days now, the students had decided which site to work on and he had meekly followed along. After they were set up and well into their routine, he would wander away and search the Boneyard. He wasn't searching for fossils, he was looking for answers. So far he hadn't found any.

He picked up another stone and balanced it in the palm of his hand. The landscape was just as barren as it was last month. The sandstone formations just as fascinating. Mother Earth had just as many dinosaurs buried beneath her surface; all it would take was someone inquisitive enough to dig them up and discover their secrets. Everything was the same as it always had been. So why wasn't he chipping away at the hardened crust? Why didn't he care if the boulder he was perched on was sitting on top of the greatest find known to science? Why was Gus the only important thing in his life and not his work? The answer came as he hurled the stone against the boulder. Because the fossils would be here tomorrow, next week, or next year. They weren't going anywhere, but Gus was.

He glanced up at a soaring vulture. Could he walk away from his dream to follow Gus back to Georgia? He chucked another rock at the boulder. Yes, he could leave the Boneyard and follow Gus to Outer Mongolia if necessary. Sometime during the past weeks she had snuck into his heart and held it captive. He had fallen in love with her.

Garrison chuckled at the simplicity of it all. Why hadn't he thought of that before? It probably would still be evading him if she hadn't mentioned it. She had said it was all right to be a little overprotective of the ones you love. Was she speaking from experience? Was she overprotective of him? Was that why she had been so frantic the other night, thinking something had happened to him? Or had she known all along what he had been hiding from himself?

The one emotion he had never thought he'd feel was smacking him straight in the face and he'd never seen it coming. He was in love with Gus! The forever, till-death-do-us-part, white wedding, and having babies kind of love. The Boneyard was to become a thing of his past. Gus had done a very admirable job coping with camp life and the personal sacrifices the Boneyard demanded, but raising a family out here three months out of the year was unheard of. Georgia had plenty of universities, and there had to be dinosaur remains somewhere in the state.

He swept up a handful of stones. He had to give Gus credit, the lady had shown more gumption than ten paleontologists combined. He had known paleontologists who whined from the day they set up camp until they returned to the hallowed air-conditioned halls of some university. She had never once complained about the food, the heat, or the lack of privacy. He pitched the first stone at the boulder—strike one.

A guilty flush swept up his jaw as he remembered the way he had treated her the night they'd thought she was lost. He should have known she was capable of finding her way back to camp on her own. Not only had she told him she knew how, but she had demonstrated it in numerous ways over the weeks. Augusta Faye Bodine could take care of herself. So why hadn't he believed her? He pitched the second stone—strike two.

Part of his doubt stemmed from arrogant thinking. He hadn't been the one to train her, so she obviously didn't know what she was doing. And the second part was more appalling than the first; he had been comparing Gus to his ex-fiancée, Catherine. The third stone smacked the boulder. Strike three and he was out.

Catherine was beautiful, all sleek lines and fluid grace. She had been sophisticated, intelligent, and worldly. But, unlike Gus, Catherine painted on a lady's face for the world to see. Gus was one hundred percent lady clean on through. She was a lady where it counted the most, on the inside.

Gus had handled the Boneyard with grace and style. The first thing he was going to do when he got back to camp was apologize for ever doubting her. It was going to take some heavy explaining on his part, but he was confident Gus would at least give him a fair hearing. Hadn't she already forgiven the students? After they straightened out that misunderstanding, he would declare his undying love and demand her hand in marriage. Once the word yes passed her lips, he was going to make love to her until the first snow fell.

He looked up and studied the sun. He still had a couple of hours of daylight left before returning to camp. With an impatient growl he stood up and strapped on the backpack. The hell with it. He was the boss, and if he couldn't say everyone could knock off a couple of hours early, then who could? He shifted the backpack against his sweat-soaked back and made a mental note to take a shower before proposing to Gus. He couldn't court her properly with candlelight dinners and flowers, but he could at least smell clean. His step quickened as he headed in the students' direction. He couldn't wait until he saw Gus.

Garrison topped the last ridge before camp a good quarter mile ahead of the students. He was on the home stretch, and Gus had better batten down the hatches, because he wasn't taking no for an answer. The hour-and-a-half-long hike back to camp had only increased his determination that Gus would belong to him forever. Whatever their differences were, they could be worked out.

He half slid and half ran down the last hill. The camper was in sight. His eyes squinted as he raised his hand to shield them from the sun. The gleam from the sun bounced off the chrome of a strange vehicle. Someone was visiting the camp. He scanned the camp and quickened his steps into a jog. No one was in sight. Lord, where was Gus? He never should have left her alone at the camp.

Garrison entered the camp and came to a screeching halt as Bertram Fremont waltzed out of the mess tent. What was he doing here? The dean never visited the Boneyard. One answer flared to life—Gus's grandfather had come to take her away! Garrison placed his hands on his hips, spread his legs apart, and prepared to take on the hardest fight of his life. "You can't take her, Fremont."

The dean slowly shook his head. "Did you say something, Fisher?"

"I said Gus isn't going back with you."

The dean's eyebrow rose at the use of the nickname. He dug into his perfectly creased dress slacks and removed a pristine white handkerchief. His only concession to the heat had been the removal of his suit jacket and the loosening of his tie. He removed his glasses and inspected a fleck of dust on a lens before wiping them clean.

His voice took on the refined quality that sent the department heads into a panic. "Whom are you referring to?"

"You know damn well *whom* I'm referring to. Your granddaughter."

Bertram continued to study the now-immaculate glasses in his hand. "And precisely where would I be taking her?"

Garrison didn't like the smile lurking around the dean's mouth. The man wanted to play games, and he wasn't in the mood. He had to find Gus and make her listen to reason. She couldn't leave the Boneyard, at least not without him. "I don't care where she wanted to go. She's not going."

"And precisely, young man, what right do you have to dictate where my granddaughter may or may not go?"

Garrison felt himself bristle at being labeled a young man. At thirty-six, one would think he deserved some respect. "Because I'm the man who . . . um . . ." He couldn't blurt out that he was going to become the dean's grandson-in-law. "I'm the man who . . ."

"Yes?" Augusta stood in the mess tent's opening, eyeing the exchange between two of her favorite men. She was very interested in hearing Garrison's response.

Garrison's gaze shifted to her at the sound of her voice. She stood glowing and radiant in the afternoon's sunlight. The pink T-shirt and denim shorts clung to her every curve. She had removed the floppy hat, but her hair was still piled up on top of her head, exposing her enticing neck. This was the only woman in the world he would willingly give up the Boneyard for. She was more than breathtaking, she was his, and he loved her. He shook a finger at her and commanded, "You're not going anywhere."

Augusta batted her eyelashes and sighed, "Lord, have mercy. I just love it when a man gets all macho and demanding on me."

The dean coughed and polished the lenses of his glasses again.

Garrison frowned and pushed his hat off his head. That didn't come out right. What had happened to the flowery speech he had rehearsed all the way back into camp? What had happened to his apology first, then a marriage proposal? He glared at the dean. It was all his fault. If he hadn't shown up, Gus would have been lying underneath him saying yes to happily-ever-after by now. He took a deep breath and smiled the little-boy smile that Gus had once told him melted her knees. "I'm sorry for snapping, Gus. Would you please reconsider and stay?"

Augusta felt her knees tremble at his smile. Garrison wanted something, and he wanted it bad. "Sure, I'll stay."

Garrison's mouth fell open in astonishment. His lady had agreed to stay without an argument. "You will?"

The dean went into a coughing fit and nearly dropped his glasses.

Augusta smiled. Garrison was still off balance, and she liked him like that. "Sure. I wasn't planning on going anywhere anyhow."

"You weren't?"

"Nope."

Garrison glared at the dean, who had seemed on the verge of an asthma attack, he had been laughing so. "Then what the hell is he doing here?"

"Garrison, that's no way to talk to my grandfather."

"Or the dean of the university that employs you," Bertram added.

"The grandfather connection I can't touch, but as for the university, I quit."

Augusta's and Bertram's voices rose in unison. "Quit?"

"In nine days I'll be leaving the Boneyard for good." He was quite proud of the way he said that, his voice barely cracking on the word *Boneyard.*

Augusta remained mute with shock as Bertram demanded, "Where in the tarnation are you going to?"

Garrison smiled at Gus. "Georgia," he said, tacking on "sir," for her sake. The old man was about to become his grandfather-in-law.

"What's in Georgia?" Bertram demanded.

Garrison took a step toward Gus. "My wife."

Augusta's mouth formed a perfect O. Garrison's finger softly caressed her bottom lip. Love radiated from her every pore. "Was that a proposal?"

"Was that a yes?"

She shook her head but continued to smile. "I can't accept under those conditions."

He scowled. "I don't remember setting any conditions." He might be a tad overprotective when it came to her safety, but he wasn't stupid enough to lay down conditions on a marriage proposal.

"We won't be living in Georgia."

"We won't?"

"Nope, I have my heart set on a house not too far from the university in Missoula."

"You do, huh." His scowl disappeared. "What else is your heart set on?"

"Four kids. Two boys and two girls."

Garrison raised an eyebrow at her determination. "I'll do my best to perform." He chuckled when a faint blush swept up her cheeks. "Anything else?"

"A summer house."

"A summer house?"

"Yes, you know, walls, kitchen, bathroom, etcetera. A place where we can go for the entire summer when you're not teaching."

If a summer home would make Gus happy, hell, he'd build it himself. "Where would you like this home; the wilds of Canada, the Carolina coast, what about southern California?"

"No."

"Then where? Just name the spot."

"You're standing on it."

Garrison looked down at his feet and thundered, "The Boneyard! You want to build a house in the Boneyard?"

Augusta held her ground. "It doesn't have to be a house, it could be a cabin or even one of those mobile homes. Don't get me wrong, I'm perfectly content with the camper, but it will get awfully crowded in there after the babies start to come."

"Babies! You would bring our babies to live out here?"

"Only for three months of the year. Think of it as a learning experience for them."

"I'll be too busy thinking of all the things that

could happen to them or you." He ran his palm across his whiskers. "Wouldn't you prefer a summer cabin in the Rockies?"

"No, there are grizzly bears in the Rockies."

"There are rattlesnakes here!"

"It would always be something, Garrison." She held her breath and waited.

She was right. No matter where they lived, there would always be something to cause him to worry about her and the babies. Good Lord, four babies to constantly worry about. Hadn't he heard a colleague once mention that if there was trouble within a hundred miles, a toddler would find it. Garrison could feel the once-dark hair by his temples slowly turning gray. "What if I say no Boneyard?"

She took a deep breath. He hadn't totally vetoed the idea. "There's one other thing my heart desires, Garrison, and that is you. I fell in love with all of you, the professor, the paleontologist, and the lover. I wouldn't be cheated out of any part of you. I want it all."

Garrison's heart exploded with joy. She said she loved him. He swept her up into his arms and ignored the round of applause the students were giving them. "I will probably drive you crazy with rules, precautions, and my constant worrying."

She wrapped her arms around his neck and held on for dear life. "I'll let you know when you become a pain."

"I'm sure you will." He started toward the camper but stopped when he noticed Newman and some other man standing by the mess tent. He and Gus had attracted an audience; so far the only ones missing were the Elisons and Hoffman, but he was sure the kids would fill them in on all details.

He bowed toward Newman and the dean. "If you would excuse us, a man likes to propose to his future wife in private." He strolled over to the camper, opened the screen door, and called over his shoulder, "Don't hold up dinner on account of us."

Augusta chuckled as they entered the camper. The look on her grandfather's face was precious. He had been torn between outrage and laughter.

"Who was that man with Newman?" Garrison's lips played against her throat.

"Oh, my!"

"That's a funny name, oh, my."

"Garrison, put me down, we have to go back outside."

He nipped at the delicate lobe of her ear. "You would rather I make love with you in front of everyone?"

"No." She tried pushing him away and wiggling out of his arms. "Don't you realize who that was?"

"You just told me his name was oh, my." He didn't care if the President of the United States was standing outside, he wasn't letting her go. The past three days had been the longest of his life.

"His name is Duncan, and he's from Chicago." Her breath was coming in small gasps as Garrison continued his assault. "He's from the MacArthur Foundation."

He continued to nibble on the highly sensitive area behind her ear. "That's nice."

"Didn't you hear me, Garrison? I said he was

from the MacArthur Foundation." Her mind was going fuzzy with desire. She couldn't think straight. "He's here to see you about a possible grant for you and the university."

Garrison stopped his tender onslaught and studied her face. "If it's that important to you, I'll see him later tonight."

"Isn't it important to you?"

"No, Gus. You're the most important thing in my life."

She smiled and snuggled closer. "Am I?"

He closed and locked the camper door. "Oh, lady, wait until I show you just how important."

Epilogue

Garrison glanced up from the papers spread out across the coffee table as Gus entered the room. "Is she asleep?"

Augusta stretched. "Finally." She leaned against an overstuffed chair and sighed as Garrison came up behind her and started to massage her lower back. "The trek through the Boneyard tired her out." His gifted hands eased the pressure. "No one can say she's not her father's daughter."

He nuzzled her neck with a kiss. "She's a natural, all right. Did you see the way her eyes lit up when she found the tooth?"

Gus chuckled. "But does she have to sleep with it under her pillow?" She sighed in contentment. Garrison had magic in his fingertips. "You knew it was there all along. If I had to guess, I'd say you planted it there for her to find."

"Hey, give Courtney a break, she's only two." His massaging fingers turned to sensual from therapeutic. "And how's the mama after her trek through the Boneyard?" His palms slid around and tenderly cupped the gentle swell of her abdomen. Their second child was starting to make his appearance known. "We're going to have to add on next summer." The mobile home he had bought Gus as a wedding present and hooked up in the middle of the Boneyard had only two bedrooms.

"I'm stiff, dirty, and in need of a bath."

The small catch in her voice alerted Garrison. "As in bubble bath?"

"Ummm . . ." She leaned back against him as his hands slid under her baggy top and cupped her tender breasts. Pregnancy had not only enlarged them but heightened their sensitivity. Heat coiled through her with just his merest touch. "You did say Ben and the students will be arriving tomorrow, didn't you?" They still had the rest of the day to themselves and Courtney. She was happy now that she had talked Garrison into coming out a few days earlier.

Garrison brushed the ponytail aside and pressed his lips to the rapidly beating pulse in her neck. "Who's Ben?"

"Your assistant," Augusta replied. "Remember you and the university hired him two years ago."

"Nice kid," he muttered against the creamy smoothness of her neck.

"He's not a kid. He's twenty-six and has every female at the university fantasizing about him."

Garrison released the front clasp of her bra. Sure fingers smoothed the lacy material away and gently stroked her breasts. "I have a few fantasies of my own." His fingers lightly squeezed the hard nipples pressing into his palms. "You did say bubbles, didn't you?"

Augusta arched deeper into his hands. "Hundreds of them." She felt the bulge in his jeans pressing against her bottom. "Thousands." Her breath caught as he softly plucked at the nubs. "Make it millions of them."

Garrison chuckled as he swung her up into his arms and carried her down the hall toward the bathroom.

She wrapped her arms around his neck and nipped at his ear. "Full speed ahead, and man the torpedoes."

THE EDITOR'S CORNER

Next month's lineup sizzles with BAD BOYS, heroes who are too hot to handle but too sinful to resist. In six marvelous romances, you'll be held spellbound by these men's deliciously wicked ways and daring promises of passion. Whether they're high-powered attorneys, brash jet jockeys, or modern-day pirates, BAD BOYS are masters of seduction who never settle for anything less than what they want. And the heroines learn that surrender comes all too easily when the loving is all too good. . . .

Fighter pilot Devlin MacKenzie in **MIDNIGHT STORM** by Laura Taylor, LOVESWEPT #576, is the first of our BAD BOYS. He and David Winslow, the hero of DESERT ROSE, LOVESWEPT #555, flew together on a mission that ended in a horrible crash, and now Devlin has come to Jessica Cleary's inn to recuperate. She broke their engagement years before, afraid to love a man who lives dangerously, but the rugged warrior changes her mind in a scorchingly sensual courtship. Laura turns up the heat in this riveting romance.

SHAMELESS, LOVESWEPT #577, by Glenna McReynolds, is the way Colt Haines broke Sarah Brooks's heart by leaving town without a word after the night she'd joyfully given him her innocence. Ten years later a tragedy brings him back to Rock Creek, Wyoming. He vows not to stay, but with one look at the woman she's become, he's determined to make her understand why he'd gone—and to finally make her his. Ablaze with the intensity of Glenna's writing, **SHAMELESS** is a captivating love story.

Cutter Beaumont *is* an **ISLAND ROGUE**, LOVESWEPT #578, by Charlotte Hughes, and he's also the mayor, sheriff, and owner of the Last Chance Saloon. Ellie Parks isn't interested though. She's come to the South Carolina island looking for a peaceful place to silence the demons that haunt her dreams—and instead she finds a handsome rake who wants to keep her up nights. Charlotte masterfully resolves this trouble in paradise with a series of events that will make you laugh and cry.

Jake Madison is nothing but **BAD COMPANY** for Nila Shepherd in Theresa Gladden's new LOVESWEPT, #579. When his sensual gaze spots her across the casino, Jake knows he must possess the temptress in the come-and-get-me dress. Nila has always wanted to walk on the wild side, but the fierce desire Jake awakens in her has her running for cover. Still, there's no hiding from this man who makes it his mission to fulfill her fantasies. Theresa just keeps coming up with terrific romances, and aren't we lucky?

Our next LOVESWEPT, #580 by Olivia Rupprecht, has one of the best titles ever—**HURTS SO GOOD**. And legendary musician Neil Grey certainly knows about hurting; that's why he dropped out of the rat race and now plays only in his New Orleans bar. Journalist Andrea Post would try just about anything to uncover his mystery, to write the story no one ever had, but the moment he calls her *"chère,"* he steals her heart. Another memorable winner from Olivia!

Suzanne Forster's stunning contribution to the BAD BOYS month is **NIGHT OF THE PANTHER**, LOVESWEPT #581. Johnny Starhawk is a celebrated lawyer whose killer instincts and Irish-Apache heritage have made him a star, but he's never forgotten the woman who'd betrayed him. And now, when Honor Bartholomew is forced to seek his help, will he give in to his need for revenge . . . or his love for the only woman he's ever wanted? This romance of smoldering anger and dangerous desire is a tour de force from Suzanne.

On sale this month from FANFARE are four terrific novels. **DIVINE EVIL** is the most chilling romantic suspense novel yet from best-selling author Nora Roberts. When successful sculptor Clare Kimball returns to her hometown, she discovers that there's a high price to pay for digging up the secrets of the past. But she finds an ally in the local sheriff, and together they confront an evil all the more terrifying because those who practice it believe it is divine.

HAVING IT ALL by critically acclaimed author Maeve Haran is a tender, funny, and revealing novel about a woman who does have it all—a glittering career, an exciting husband, and two adorable children. But she tires of pretending she's superwoman, and her search for a different kind of happiness and success shocks the family and friends she loves.

With **HIGHLAND FLAME**, Stephanie Bartlett brings back the beloved heroine of HIGHLAND REBEL. In this new novel, Catriona Galbraid and her husband, Ian, depart Scotland's Isle of Skye after they're victorious in their fight for justice for the crofters. But when a tragedy leaves Cat a widow, she's thrust into a new struggle—and into the arms of a new love.

Talented Virginia Lynn creates an entertaining variation on the taming-of-the-shrew theme with **LYON'S PRIZE**. In medieval England the Saxon beauty Brenna of Marwald is forced to marry Rye de Lyon, the Norman knight known as the Black Lion. She vows that he will never have her love, but he captures her heart with passion.

Sharon and Tom Curtis are among the most talented authors of romantic fiction, and you wouldn't want to miss this chance to pick up a copy of their novel **THE GOLDEN TOUCH**, which LaVyrle Spencer has praised as being "pure pleasure!" This beautifully written romance has two worlds colliding when an internationally famous pop idol moves into the life of a small-town teacher.

The Delaneys are coming! Once again Kay Hooper, Iris Johansen, and Fayrene Preston have collaborated to bring you a sparkling addition to this remarkable family's saga. Look for **THE DELANEY CHRISTMAS CAROL**— available soon from FANFARE.

Happy reading!

With best wishes,

Nita Taublib
Associate Publisher
LOVESWEPT and FANFARE

DIVINE EVIL
by the *New York Times* bestselling author of
CARNAL INNOCENCE and GENUINE LIES,
NORA ROBERTS

Sculptor Clare Kimball has a dynamic, individualistic style that set the New York art world on end. But as Clare travels back to her tiny home town of Emmitsboro, Maryland, she must confront the tragedy of her father's suicide and the half-remembered nightmares that suggest Clare, as a small child, was the witness to terrible acts that give the lie to Emmitsboro's image of homespun "niceness." Will Clare's presence trigger fear—and retaliation—in those who know more than they're saying about the town's dark side? Clare's only ally is Cameron Rafferty, the high school bad-boy turned sheriff. The wary curiosity Clare feels toward Cam turns quickly into something else—a white-hot desire and an unwelcome love. In Cam's arms Clare tells herself she is safe. But Clare will pay a price for digging up the secrets of the past—and will confront an evil all the more terrifying because those who practice it believe it is divine.

HAVING IT ALL
by
Maeve Haran

With a glittering career that will soon make her the most powerful woman in British television, an exciting marriage, and two adorable children, Liz Ward has everything she's always wanted . . . and no time to enjoy it. Tired of missing out on bedtime stories, family dinner, and slow sex, Liz decides to stop glossing over the guilt and panic of trying to do it all. She's going to find a new way to get the happiness and success she wants, on her own terms. But it's a search that will send shock waves not only through her life but through the lives of the family and friends that she loves.

"Funny, poignant and true . . . reveals everything we won't admit about being a working woman." —Rosie Thomas, author of ALL MY SINS REMEMBERED.

A British bestseller in its first American edition.

HIGHLAND FLAME
by
Stephanie Bartlett
author of
HIGHLAND REBEL

In this stand-alone "sequel" to HIGHLAND REBEL, Catriona Galbraith and her beloved husband Ian depart Scotland's Isle of

Skye after their fight to win justice for the crofters is victorious. But when tragedy leaves Cat a widow, she is thrust into a new struggle—a battle between Texas farmers and the railroads—and swept by fate into passion more powerful than she'd ever known. Can the dreams that died with Ian be reborn in a new land and in the arms of a new love?

Will hesitated at the foot of the steps to his office, breathing in the dusty sweetness of the autumn twilight. Catriona hadn't wanted to leave Geordie, but the lad rode off alone into the prairie. Will had insisted on driving Catriona into Arlington to the mortician. Knowing how she'd acted when Ian died, he was surprised when she agreed.

Will knew he ought to go on to the livery, get the buggy, and drive Catriona home as he'd promised. But somehow he just couldn't bear the thought of leaving her there and driving back to town alone. As they stood together on the plank sidewalk, the weight of her hand on his arm was his only link to life, to sanity. She understood his sense of loss as no one else ever could. He cleared his throat and turned to her. "I—would you be insulted if I suggested stopping at the office for a few minutes? I keep a bottle of whiskey there, and I think we could both use a drink."

Her lovely face turned up toward his, drawn and pale from their long ordeal, but marked by an odd calm. "Aye, I could use a taste at that."

He guided her up the steep steps and unlocked the door, fumbling inside for a lamp and a match. Air warmed by the afternoon sun surrounded him with familiar scents of leather and carbolic as the wick caught and a circle of light flared around them. Carrying the lamp, he led the way into his private office. He set the light on a corner of the desk and pulled up an armchair for Catriona.

She dropped into it with a delicate sigh, leaning her head against the high back and closing her eyes.

He seated himself in the desk chair, then delved in the bottom desk drawer for the flask. The cork rolled to a stop on the thick green blotter, and he poured an inch of the brownish liquor in the only glass and set it in front of Cat. He tipped the bottle to his lips, savoring the trail of fire burning all the way to his belly.

But even that couldn't erase the image of Molly stretched across the bed she'd shared with Geordie, a child dying giving birth to another child. What kind of world was it where such things could happen?

He stood and paced to the window, seeing but not seeing the molten gold of the sunset spreading across the horizon, drawing starry darkness down after it. Sudden frustration surged through him at the senselessness and waste, at his own helplessness. All his skill hadn't saved her. There was just too much he didn't know. He pitched the flask with all his might against the wall. It crashed, showering fragments of glass and drops of whiskey onto the wooden floor. "Goddammit, I shouldn't have let them die!"

Catriona turned her tear-stained face, eyes wide and her mouth open. After a moment her lips set in a grim line and her eyes narrowed. "And who would you be to decide that? God himself? Face it, man, you couldna save them. No one could."

Her words arrowed into him, through all the scars, the years of armor, opening all the wounds anew. Tears burned a trail of acid down his face. And now he must add shame, the shame of showing his impotence before this woman, the woman he cared more about than anyone else in the world. He sank down into the chair and turned his face away, unwilling to look into her accusing eyes.

Then suddenly her arms were around him, pressing his face to the soft warmth of her bosom. Her kindness dissolved what was left of his calm. He pressed against her, letting the tears flow, losing himself in his grief. Nothing would bring back Molly or her son, or Ian, or a host of others he'd lost through the years. He'd become a doctor to save lives, without ever counting the cost of those he failed to save.

Catriona was right—he was only a man, not a god. He'd done his best, all he could do, and it was time to stop carrying around the ghosts of those who'd died in his care. At last, after he'd spent the grief of years, the tears stopped and he sat for a moment, enjoying a deep sense of peace.

Then a slow awareness returned. He held a woman in his arms, a woman he'd dreamed of holding, a woman he loved. Without loosening his arms he leaned back in her embrace and turned his face up toward hers.

Tears jeweled her dark lashes, and her soft lips trembled, but something more than pain or compassion hid in her dark blue eyes.

Desire flamed through him as he stood and cupped her face in both hands. Beyond thought, he bent and pressed his lips to hers, breathing in the mystery of her woman-musk.

With a soft groan she wound her arms around his neck, and he drew her to him, marveling at the softness of her breasts, her belly, her thighs pressing against him. With a sigh he released her, then scooped her in his arms and carried her to the cot in the corner.

The narrow bed protested at the weight pressing down on it. Catriona sank back into the softness, floating in an urgency of desire. She clung to his lips, drinking in his kisses, greedy for the whiskey taste of his mouth, his tongue. His mouth burned kisses down her throat.

Passion smoldered low in her belly, a delicious agony of fire longing to be quenched. One hand molded her skirt over her hips and down her thighs. His voice whispered out of the darkness. "Catriona, are you sure?"

A giddy joy, almost laughter, bubbled up in her. "Aye, never more than now."

Hunger possessed her as he ran the tips of his fingers over her back, her breasts, her belly.

She pressed her face against his shoulder. All the hidden longing of the last year welled up in her. As she melted against him, his lips sought hers in a gentle communion. He stretched his body beside hers. Pulling her against him, he curled around her, one spoon nestled against another, whispering her name. "Catriona, I love you."

LYON'S PRIZE

by Virginia Brown writing as Virginia Lynn
author of
SUMMER'S KNIGHT, CUTTER'S WOMAN,
and RIVER'S DREAM

*From the spellbinding Virginia Lynn comes LYON'S PRIZE, a
tantalizing new historical romance with all the passion and color of
its medieval setting. A defiant young Saxon beauty has sworn to
kill the Norman knight who dares to marry her. But as we see in
the following scene, she hasn't bargained for Rye de Lyon, known
far and wide as The Black Lion for his legendary conquests at
war—and with the ladies . . .*

A burst of laughter erupted below, and Brenna's lip curled.
Damn them. Damn them all.

When she reached the small square landing at the angle of
the stairs, Brenna caught a glimpse of movement behind her.
She turned quickly, her hand moving to the small poniard at
her hip.

"Do not pull your weapon," the man said softly in the
Norman tongue, which Brenna understood as well as she did
her own.

Brenna sucked in a sharp breath. A Norman, and he
looked much too dangerous. And close. Her fingers closed
around the hilt of her dagger, and she pulled it from the
jeweled sheath in a smooth, graceful motion.

"Stay where you are," she commanded sharply in French.
"I have no intention of allowing you within a foot of me.
Stay, I said, or I'll shout for my father's guard."

"From what I saw of your father's anger at you, he would

not lift a finger to stay me," the man replied with a sardonic twist of his mouth.

Brenna felt a spasm of fear shoot through her and was annoyed by it. Afraid? Of this man? Of *any* man? She jabbed the dagger in his direction.

"Stay away, or I'll slit you from gullet to gut!"

"Such sweet words, milady," the man mocked. He was only two stairs away now, and Brenna felt with her foot for the next stair up.

She looked at him closely. She did not recognize him and would have known if he'd been in Marwald before. No one could fail to remember this man.

He was tall, very tall, and his shoulders were broad, filling out the fine velvet of his tunic. A worked gold brooch held his mantle on one shoulder, and the hem swirled around lean, muscled legs. A broadsword hung from a wide leather belt at his side, seeming out of place with the elegant clothes, yet fitting for a man with such a hard face. Brenna felt a thrum of apprehension. A scar raked his face from eyebrow to cheekbone, slender and curved, giving his dark countenance an even more dangerous appearance. Beneath winged black brows, eyes of a startling blue pierced the air between them, thick-lashed and assessing.

There was an unholy beauty about him, a silent promise of ruthless determination and masculine appeal that made her throat tighten. She stared at him without blinking, fascinated in spite of herself.

"Do you approve, milady?" came the slightly mocking question, delivered in a husky voice.

Brenna straightened immediately. "Whoreson," she muttered in English before demanding in the French language he would understand, "Who are you? What do you want with me?"

By this time the man had reached the step where she stood, and she felt his proximity like a blow. Every nerve in her body screamed at her to flee, but she refused to act a coward. Particularly not before this mocking coxcomb with his fine clothes and neatly cropped hair.

"I want you, *demoiselle*."

Brenna stared at him. Her throat tightened as if a hand had closed around it. For a moment she thought she might actually faint. No. Not this man. He looked too hard, too savage. He did not look at all like a man who would be turned away with a few scornful words. It would take a great deal to turn this Norman knight from his purpose, she realized.

For the first time in years, Brenna was truly afraid of a man. She steeled herself. She could not let him know it. It would be fatal.

Her laugh rippled through the air, and she clutched her dagger tightly at the slight narrowing of his eyes. "Do you want me, sir? How very unfortunate for you." Edging up a step at a time, Brenna put some distance between them. She was not deceived by the man's seeming indolence. There was something about his pose that suggested a coiled spring. He was likely to leap on her without warning.

She reached the top step and flung back her head in defiance. "You won't have me, Sir Knight."

"I always get what I want."

It lay between them, that softly spoken statement, as certain and confident as sunrise. Brenna's mouth felt suddenly dry, and her heart slammed against her ribs. Yea, she'd been right. This man was dangerous.

"I'm afraid, sir, that you are doomed to disappointment this time." Her smile flashed briefly and falsely. "I do not wish to wed."

"That is of no importance to me." He moved at last, his powerful body shifting gracefully up the next stair. "Your king and your father have decreed that you will wed."

"And I do not obey lightly, sir." Brenna felt the last step at her heel, and took it. When she saw him move toward her again, she lashed out with the dagger, catching the velvet sleeve of his tunic and slashing it. Her heart was pounding with fear, and she hoped her legs did not give way beneath her. This man had not moved to avoid the blade, nor to catch her arm. He seemed completely indifferent to the threat she posed, and that was as infuriating as it was frightening.

"Get back!" she said sharply. She was no novice with a dagger; to amuse themselves, her brothers had taught her to fight. Now the lessons stood her in good stead, and she balanced on the balls of her feet as she faced this bold-eyed Norman. "Are you a fool to brave my blade?"

A smile curled his mouth, but didn't reach his eyes. "You toy with a dagger. When you think to become serious, I will take it from you."

None of her disquiet showed in her voice when she spat, "I am serious now."

"And would you stab me before the wedding?"

"Yea. I would slit you from navel to chin with no less haste," she hissed at him.

"Then do it, *demoiselle.*" This time the smile reached his eyes, and he moved closer.

Brenna stared at him uncertainly. Perhaps he didn't believe that she really would use the dagger on him. He wouldn't be the first to feel the bite of her steel. There had been the overeager suitor who'd thought to dishonor her, thus forcing her into a marriage. He'd worn bandages on his arm for a month after. Now this bold man *dared* her to do it.

"I will," she said softly, and felt the hilt of her poniard slide reassuringly against her palm. "I've no love for Normans. Nay, I've no love for any man. 'Twould give me great pleasure to do what you seem to think I won't."

"Not won't." Amusement glittered in cold blue eyes, the exotic eyes of the devil. "Can't."

Stung, Brenna swung the dagger up, intending to slash his other sleeve and maybe draw a bit of blood along with it, just to show him.

To her astonishment the dagger was sent skittering down the steps in a clatter of metal and bone, and the Norman was gripping her wrist so tightly she gasped with the pain of it.

"Let go of me . . ."

"Aye, lady." He dragged her slowly to him. "When I'm through with you."

His face was only inches from hers, and she had no warning of what he intended until his dark head bent and he grazed her lips with his mouth. Stunned into immobile fury, Brenna couldn't think for a moment. He dared kiss her without asking permission! Few had done that and gone away unmarked, and neither would this Norman.

THE GOLDEN TOUCH
by Sharon and Tom Curtis
authors of
SUNSHINE AND SHADOW

"Ahhh, pure pleasure! . . . [THE GOLDEN TOUCH] is as tempting as one fresh, warm cookie from the oven—every page! Just couldn't get enough."

—LaVyrle Spencer

THE GOLDEN TOUCH is an amazingly beautiful story from America's most beloved romance writing team. This tale of impossible love between a small-town widow and a famous rock star reverberates with profound emotions and will tug at every one of your heart strings. In the following scene, Kathy Carter is quietly minding her musical instrument repair shop when her life suddenly changes . . .

She saw the motorcycle flash by her window and then heard it revving for a moment before it stopped down the street. *Someone thinks they're James Dean. What a royal pain in the neck.* Kathy rested her head in her hands.

She looked up when the door jingled. It was obviously the rider of the motorcycle—evident from the sand-colored suede bomber jacket and the helmet with a smoked glass visor he was pulling from his head. *Oh, no.* She knew it was just one of those silly small-town prejudices, but for her motorcyclists had a bad image based on old Marlon Brando movies where small towns like Apple Grove were destroyed by leather-jacketed hoodlums. He seemed to have a pack slung on his back.

But if the man in the leather jacket had mayhem on his mind, it was well hidden under the half-smile that was curving on his face. Specimens like that didn't make a habit of walking into "Kathy's Instrument Repair." Somewhere in the back of her mind, Kathy was surprised to feel a tiny synapse that meant that somehow she recognized him. Try as she would, she couldn't place the man. He was older than she—perhaps in his late twenties. Could he be one of her old friends from high school? Someone she'd been introduced to at summer camp? At college? Impossible. None of the possibilities rode motorcycles or wore leather. And the face before her was not one she would have forgotten readily.

He had nice features, though he wasn't what she'd call male-model, pose-for-perfume ads handsome. His face had too much character in it for that, and a glint of humor that hinted he didn't take himself too seriously. In a world filled with tension and pomposity, that quality was intently compelling. Dangerous. His hair was deep brown, full-bodied and shining. It was cleverly cut and longish, with an enchanting bedroom disarray from the helmet.

His cheekbones were high and wide-set, his jaw firm, and there was a tiny scar on his cleft chin. There was nothing particularly remarkable about his build—it was just the right amount slim and gracefully put together, though his shoulders had a look of strength to them. Good grief, why was she thinking about his body?

Feeling embarrassed, she raised her eyes quickly to his. They were pale blue—but, oh, what a pale blue, with an inner brightness, a calm study to them that was focused, just now, on her face. Instantly, she was taken aback. The man looked as though he could read every thought that passed through her head. Kathy didn't often find herself at a loss with someone, but to her dismay, she felt rather intimidated. She hoped none of that showed on the surface. Her hand strayed self-consciously to the straggling curls on her forehead. She lowered it quickly. Shape up, Kathy girl.

He had let her study him with a certain cool and rather amused patience. In fact, it seemed disconcertingly as though he were accustomed to that kind of survey. Then, as if he sensed that she had completed her catalogue of his features, he lifted the shoulder strap over his head. In the silhouetting light from the window, she saw that he held a battered guitar.

"I've got a problem," he said. "Maybe you'll be able to help me?"

The words might be ordinary, but the man in front of Kathy had an extraordinary voice. It was one beat quicker than a drawl, and marked by a delicately sexual rasp that licked its way into her body through the spine. She watched him lay his guitar on the counter, his voice echoing through her like the memory of a caress. Good Lord! What made her think that? All at once it occurred to her that she couldn't remember what he'd said to her. The effect of his voice had been so intense that the content of his words escaped her.

"Please?" she said automatically, meaning "I beg your pardon?" It was a central Illinois usage Kathy had picked up in childhood from her mother.

"Please?" he repeated quizzically. Then, correctly interpreting an idiom that was obviously unfamiliar to him, he said, "Oh, I see. Can you replace the tuning peg?" The voice again, a warm handstroke on her heart.

He lifted the neck of the guitar and showed her the broken peg.

The way a parent responds to a youngster with a scraped knee was exactly the way Kathy responded to a damaged musical instrument. She stood up, too quickly, and at the same time realized who she'd just said "please" to. She'd seen his face on Marijo Johnson's chest. She'd heard his luxuriant voice on her old gray radio.

"Neil Stratton," she said. Black spots shot into her eyes, spots that turned red, then green. Retreating blood prickled in her fingertips, and a hundredweight of dizziness spread its rapidly intensifying pressure under her skull. Heartsick and humiliated, she thought, Oh God, why didn't I eat? I'm going to faint! And she did.

Which was how Kathy Allison Carter, small-town instrument-repair technician and piano teacher, happened to wake up in the arms of Neil Stratton, songwriter, musician, and celebrity of international repute.

Regaining consciousness was an unpleasant business that was like swimming to the surface of a heavily chlorinated pool after taking a belly flop from the high board. She was short of breath, her legs felt numb, and her eyes itched. Opening them with a few blinks, Kathy found she was lying on the old burgundy floral couch in her back room with Neil Stratton supporting her in one arm and gently applying a warm terry washcloth to her temples with the other.

"Could you drink a little?" asked the wonderful voice.

She nodded weakly. The hand with the washcloth left her face and returned in a moment with a paper cup, which was pressed lightly to her lower lip. Sipping the water, she became slowly more aware of his hard-muscled arm where it made warm contact with her back through the thin cotton of her shirt. He was so close she could feel his clean breath on her eyelashes and smell the spring breeze and leather from his collar, his hair.

After she'd fainted, he had obviously picked her up and brought her to the couch—and then what? The washcloth, the water—he must have found the washroom behind the stairs, looked in the linen closet for the washcloth, found the paper-cup dispenser behind the door. A man of resource.

"You know, I could see it if I were Elvis," he said. Kathy could hear the smile in his voice. "I don't get many swoons these days. It was charming, though, if a little old-fashioned."

Carefully, she was lowered to the couch and a lemon yellow bolster pillow slid forward to support her head. A sudden and unexpected pang of disappointment shook her as his arms withdrew from her body. Somehow, paradoxically, the most important thing in her life became to disabuse him of any notion that she had fainted because he was—well, who he was.

Mustering one's dignity is something of a challenge when one is spread flat out and disheveled on a couch, but Kathy did her best. Forcing herself, she looked straight up into the blue eyes that were studying her with such fine-honed perception. "I know how it must have looked, but it wasn't anything to do with you. I was hungry."

OFFICIAL RULES TO WINNERS CLASSIC SWEEPSTAKES

No Purchase necessary. To enter the sweepstakes follow instructions found elsewhere in this offer. You can also enter the sweepstakes by hand printing your name, address, city, state and zip code on a 3" x 5" piece of paper and mailing it to: Winners Classic Sweepstakes, P.O. Box 785, Gibbstown, NJ 08027. Mail each entry separately. Sweepstakes begins 12/1/91. Entries must be received by 6/1/93. Some presentations of this sweepstakes may feature a deadline for the Early Bird prize. If the offer you receive does, then to be eligible for the Early Bird prize your entry must be received according to the Early Bird date specified. Not responsible for lost, late, damaged, misdirected, illegible or postage due mail. Mechanically reproduced entries are not eligible. All entries become property of the sponsor and will not be returned.

Prize Selection/Validations: Winners will be selected in random drawings on or about 7/30/93, by VENTURA ASSOCIATES, INC., an independent judging organization whose decisions are final. Odds of winning are determined by total number of entries received. Circulation of this sweepstakes is estimated not to exceed 200 million. Entrants need not be present to win. All prizes are guaranteed to be awarded and delivered to winners. Winners will be notified by mail and may be required to complete an affidavit of eligibility and release of liability which must be returned within 14 days of date of notification or alternate winners will be selected. Any guest of a trip winner will also be required to execute a release of liability. Any prize notification letter or any prize returned to a participating sponsor, Bantam Doubleday Dell Publishing Group, Inc., its participating divisions or subsidiaries, or VENTURA ASSOCIATES, INC. as undeliverable will be awarded to an alternate winner. Prizes are not transferable. No multiple prize winners except as may be necessary due to unavailability, in which case a prize of equal or greater value will be awarded. Prizes will be awarded approximately 90 days after the drawing. All taxes, automobile license and registration fees, if applicable, are the sole responsibility of the winners. Entry constitutes permission (except where prohibited) to use winners' names and likenesses for publicity purposes without further or other compensation.

Participation: This sweepstakes is open to residents of the United States and Canada, except for the province of Quebec. This sweepstakes is sponsored by Bantam Doubleday Dell Publishing Group, Inc. (BDD), 666 Fifth Avenue, New York, NY 10103. Versions of this sweepstakes with different graphics will be offered in conjunction with various solicitations or promotions by different subsidiaries and divisions of BDD. Employees and their families of BDD, its division, subsidiaries, advertising agencies, and VENTURA ASSOCIATES, INC., are not eligible.

Canadian residents, in order to win, must first correctly answer a time limited arithmetical skill testing question. Void in Quebec and wherever prohibited or restricted by law. Subject to all federal, state, local and provincial laws and regulations.

Prizes: The following values for prizes are determined by the manufacturers' suggested retail prices or by what these items are currently known to be selling for at the time this offer was published. Approximate retail values include handling and delivery of prizes. Estimated maximum retail value of prizes: 1 Grand Prize ($27,500 if merchandise or $25,000 Cash); 1 First Prize ($3,000); 5 Second Prizes ($400 each); 35 Third Prizes ($100 each); 1,000 Fourth Prizes ($9.00 each) ; 1 Early Bird Prize ($5,000); Total approximate maximum retail value is $50,000. Winners will have the option of selecting any prize offered at level won. Automobile winner must have a valid driver's license at the time the car is awarded. Trips are subject to space and departure availability. Certain black-out dates may apply. Travel must be completed within one year from the time the prize is awarded. Minors must be accompanied by an adult. Prizes won by minors will be awarded in the name of parent or legal guardian.

For a list of Major Prize Winners (available after 7/30/93): send a self-addressed, stamped envelope entirely separate from your entry to: Winners Classic Sweepstakes Winners, P.O. Box 825, Gibbstown, NJ 08027. Requests must be received by 6/1/93. DO NOT SEND ANY OTHER CORRESPONDENCE TO THIS P.O. BOX.